I0546956

OMEGA UNTAMED

The Omega Misfits Book #6

by

Wendy Rathbone

Omega Untamed: The Omega Misfits Book 6
Copyright © September 2020 by Wendy Rathbone

TITLE: Omega Untamed: The Omega Misfits Book 6
Author: Wendy Rathbone
Cover by: Wendy Rathbone
ISBN: 978-1-942415-38-1

© All rights reserved. This book may not be reproduced wholly or in part without prior written permission from the publisher and author, except by a reviewer who may quote brief passages. Neither may any section of this book be reproduced, stored in a retrieval system, or transmitted in any form or by any means, electronic, mechanical, photocopying, recording or other, without prior written permission from the author, except as exempted by legitimate purchase through the author's website, Amazon.com or other authorized retailer.

Address all inquiries to the author at:
wrathbone@juno.com

Piracy ruins lives!

This book is legally copyrighted © and MAY NOT be uploaded to any electronic storage center, website, or other such device/location. Period. End of argument. We are a small, independent company – if you upload this book to an illegal download site, you are robbing my family and my cats and dogs, who really do need to eat. You know better. Please don't do it!

For Della, as always…

Special thanks to my amazing beta reader, the talented Jackie North, who is responsible for saving Kee's life. The first mention of this character is in *Omega Chattel*, Book 5 of *The Omega Misfits*. In that book, Kee is missing. I could not decide whether Kee should turn up dead or alive, but Jackie insisted that Kee, as a lost boy, has his own story to tell and must be allowed to tell it. Thus, at the end of book 5, he turns up alive.

Omega Untamed, Book 6, is Kee's story. Thank you, Jackie, for helping me see it needed to be written.

Chapter One

Kee

He might have been two hundred years old. He might have come out of the wastelands after having lived there for decades, surviving off cactus and the occasional miraculous spring. The cold starlight of that country still mirrored in his strange black eyes. He might have been wrinkled and far too somber for my tastes, but this Alpha wore a two thousand dollar silk suit and diamonds on his hands. His hair was still dark without a hint of gray—expensive dye job?—and he'd been eying me all night as if he had thousand dollar bills ready to hand me.

I laughed behind my tall, fizzy drink. Did Alphas that old still feel their Burns? What did I care as long as the guy paid? I'd do anything for pay.

"So many eyes, Kee," came a whisper in my ear.

Tobi, one of my street friends, wore a gold vest, low slung gray trousers and not much else but some hastily applied glitter on his slim form. He sashayed away, turned and grinned at me.

"Your point?" I asked.

"Everywhere you go people stare. You're a conceited slut, but you attract them like flies; I'll give you that."

I glanced around. Neon behind the bar made the bottles glow gold, green and blue. The tables were packed with hungry, broody Alphas, some looking for a good time, some on the verge of a Burn. The stage had mostly naked Omegas covered in silver or gold paint and glitter, gyrating in every possible submissive position to loud industrial music. Everything looked normal. For a pick up bar.

And yes, all eyes were on me, despite the strippers. My chest swelled with pride. I laughed again. What else was new? I knew how to play it up better than any of the dancers. Better than any street boy out there.

I could take a torn sleeveless jacket with no shirt, ragged old jeans and scuffed boots and wear them like a suit of silk. Accessorizing my smooth-muscled, tanned skin with a ring, a gold bracelet, or a choker, made me shine even more. As long as enough skin showed through the rips of my jeans in all the right places—the crease between where thigh and butt cheek met, knees, upper front thighs—and my hair fell just right against the cat-gleam of my green eyes, I had no trouble finding my way into the most posh parties in the richest homes.

Some called me beautiful. Some called me cute. But I never met an Alpha who didn't want to keep me. Own me. Tame me.

Funny, because they didn't even realize how they appeared. So needy. So greedy. Such baby boys only wanting what they wanted. They didn't know me, but they were all ready to claim me and bond me in the shackles of their power-hungry domineering lifestyles deemed normal by our culture if only I would say yes.

Fuck that.

Superior assholes who bought and sold Omegas like they were oil or copper or gems on the trade market.

Sure, I sold myself. But not for keeps. I took the money and went my way.

Most Alphas were despicable. A few were okay. The rare ones that made me bite my lip against caring a little too much were the ones I ran fastest from.

The one staring at me now with his thousand dollar bill eyes and his wrinkled face was no doubt one of the despicables. Despite his dried up appearance, seemingly heat-soaked on the beds of fire-ants for decades, he gave off an air of ice and sharpness.

Even if I charged him by the minute, some exorbitant, embarrassingly large sum, instinct assured me he'd pay it.

So I stared back.

Another Alpha caught my eye, then. Much younger. Handsomer. Taller. Wearing some strange, light-weight coat that was long at the knees and all black. I would have rather had him, but he didn't look rich. His hair was tamed straight back but a little messy on the sides, blacker than mine, and his features were also sharp, a little hardened but pretty. He'd be all angles and mutters, probably, all possessive, too.

The meaner, wrinkled one would pay more and toss me out in the morning, so he was the one I decided to court.

I played hard to get because I could. Because it was fun. I put on a show every time, let all the Alphas think they might get a taste. No matter where I was, this was my routine. Bars. Street corners. Clubs. It didn't make any difference.

Once an Alpha said to me, after he'd chained me up and had his way with me for the two days of his Burn, "You're made of gold and gall."

I had to look it up. *Gall.* Insolence. Impertinence. I laughed and laughed. I so totally could live with that.

All I could say to every Alpha I met, as long as they didn't do more than fuck me or beat me (just a little), was, "More! More!"

Orgasmic highs kept me going strong. When I came down from them, I used. My personality filled entire rooms, and when I was high I owned the world.

Or so I thought.

The strip joint bar was called Moosie's, named after the Alpha owner. Everyone called him Goosie behind his back, though, because of his pocked skin and beak-like nose. I came here often because it was so easy. Any club or street corner could be my office, but Moosie's, strangely, had the best clientele. And the best drug dealing going on in the john.

The air reeked of alcohol and cheap perfume. My elixir.

I always somehow got the center table at Moosie's, no matter how busy it was. I sat like a king while other Omegas I knew—and some I didn't—came and went.

The Omega waiters served me drink after drink, always bending down to tell me who paid for each one.

"This is from the Alpha with the red hat in the far left corner."

"This is from the Alpha by the door who keeps sneezing."

"This is from the Alpha who looks like a frog."

I would raise my glass, meet their eyes, and drink. But never get up. No. Not until I was ready. Etiquette, for me at least, was that if you were an Alpha and you wanted me for a night, you never approached me. You let me come to you.

I didn't have to advertise my rules. They were known. People talked. People talked about me. I had a reputation. People knew my name. Kee. Everywhere I went, they knew me even if we'd never met. They knew if they wanted me, they had to wait for me to choose.

Once in a while, if someone got rough, or tried to approach me and force me, the cops would be called either by a friend, me or even strangers.

One cop once said to me, "With the money you make, I suggest a bodyguard."

"I can take care of myself," I scoffed. It made me bristle to think it. That any Alpha had the right or the *gall* to make me feel in danger.

I let it be known I had powerful Alpha friends and if anyone tried anything with me, anyone I didn't *choose*, my Alphas would retaliate.

It was a lie, of course.

But it worked. The armor I had on the streets was invisible and unreal. But they didn't know that. And I had started to believe in it myself.

Tobi came by again in a cloud of whiskey breath and sweat. "You keep eying the wrinkled dude. Can it. He may look rich but he's bad news."

"I handle bad news just fine every day."

Tobi smirked.

I got a tiny bit drunk. And prettier, I guess, because more Alphas bought me drinks than I could keep up with and I started giving them away.

I coyly asking around. "What's the wrinkled guy's name?"

"Myre," said an Omega I'd never met.

"Myre? What a horrible name!"

I didn't really drink as much as I pretended. For every drink I got, I took maybe three sips, then let them melt to ice. Later, the ones I gave away never touched my lips.

I needed some wits about me to ply my trade.

But I also needed a few hits of steam to keep me going. Steam was the street word for uppers. They gave you popping energy. They made erections hard and strong and last for hours.

When I got up to go to the john, Tobi and two others trailed me, probably hoping I'd buy a lot and share. Yeah, I always did.

The dealers tonight were Marc and Stiv. I knew them well. "Hey" We slapped hands in the usual greeting. I pulled out a wad of cash.

Stiv handled the money, Marc had the merch.

"Aren't Cho and Rebel usually on Friday nights?"

Stiv grunted.

Marc shook his head.

"They get arrested or something?"

"We're not supposed to talk about that," said Marc.

"I know a few cops. Had 'em in my bed. Maybe I can put in a good word."

"Shut the fuck up," said Stiv. "You have a big mouth, you know that?" He never talked to me like that. I'd never seen him so furious.

9

"Hey, no harm, no foul." I put my hands up.

I took the steam and handed out a few small packs to my friends before pocketing the rest.

I turned to leave and felt a hand on my shoulder. Stiv was staring at me. In a low voice, he said, "You get around a lot and you talk a lot. Maybe you're the reason Cho and Rebel got snagged."

I frowned. "I don't talk about you guys. Not ever. Not to anyone."

"Keep it that way." Stiv squeezed my shoulder a little too hard, then let go.

I rolled my eyes and shook my head.

In the hall, I said aloud, "Creep!"

Maybe he heard me. Maybe not. The music blared. Everyone had their own agendas.

When I got back to the main area, past the stripper stage and the bar, I glanced around for old wrinkly-face. Myre. But he wasn't to be seen anywhere.

Before my eyes, I saw my dream of thousand dollar bills falling away to ash.

"Damn!"

I scanned the room for the Alpha in the long coat—my second choice—and he was gone as well.

My phone buzzed. It was a text from Tarin, one of at least a dozen from him in the past two weeks. He was one of the few Alphas I'd spent more than one Burn with. I hadn't seen him in many weeks, and had no plans to, but I wasn't sure how to tell him that.

Of all my partners, I truly believed Tarin when he told me he loved me. He'd offered me everything, yet never tried to change who I was. Never tried to make me stay against my will. He always let me go, his face drawn and needy, but not quite as greedy as all the others.

Tarin was a good guy and deserved better. Better than me. I ignored the text.

Tobi touched me on my back. "Thanks for the steam."

"Everything's so boring tonight," I said, raising my voice and leaning into him. I grabbed his gold vest. "Let's go somewhere else."

He nodded and turned toward the exit. I knew Tobi had a car. I could never keep one myself. It wasn't for lack of money. I could never remember to pay my bills. Ever.

In Tobi's car we could do my steam in privacy and prepare for the next club.

We came out of the bar and into cool air and the gaudy, neon lights of the Trenches. The smell of gasoline, dew-damp asphalt and rotting garbage made up the ever-persistent perfume of the streets.

"Where's your car?" I nudged Tobi with my shoulder.

"Down this way." He started walking toward a little lot in an alley alongside the bar. As we turned the corner, something slammed into my face, hard.

I started to fall when everything went dark.

Chapter Two

Bast

"Grab him! Grab him!"

I didn't think. I acted. I did as I was told. My Alpha boss usually left all organization to me unless I totally fucked up. That was the way I liked it. But tonight he was sticking his nose into this little drama as if he personally wanted hands on, something he never did.

The Omega was falling. His knees bent and I caught him under the arms before he hit the pavement.

The other who was with him went down hard and we left him there, groaning and bleeding, in the gutters of the alley.

The one in my arms was big for an Omega, lean hard muscles, tall, might've passed for an Alpha if it weren't for his peaches and cream scent.

Someone brought the Lincoln around to the mouth of the alley. Doors opened. I lifted him into the backseat without effort.

Stone, one of Myre's favorite henchmen and the one who hit the Omega got into the Lincoln's backseat from the other side. Now the Omega lay unconscious between us.

Myre got into the front passenger seat, motioning wildly with his arms. "Drive!"

The car screeched away.

I rolled my eyes. Nicely done. Way to *not* bring attention to our nocturnal activities.

But it wasn't my business. None of it was. *Don't think. Just act.* It had been my motto for two years.

We'd all been informed of the Omega named Kee, wild, untamable. An addict. He was too easy with his ways. He bragged. Supposedly he talked too much. Namely, about who he bought his drugs from.

Two days ago, two of Myre's soldiers had been arrested. Talk around the Trenches was it was Kee who'd tipped off the cops. Whether intentionally or not, didn't matter. It was well-known Kee had cop friends he serviced, and who in turn helped look after him.

Myre had had enough of this brash Omega who ran savage over Alpha hearts for top dollar hyped up on sex and drugs, and name-dropped every chance he got.

Privately, I thought Kee was good for business. And I knew he wasn't the one who'd ratted. But then again, I didn't get paid to think. Never. No thought. Just to the job.

Kee's weight pressed against my shoulder, his head lolling side to side, his mouth slightly open. I couldn't help but notice his extreme beauty. No Alpha could help it. The firm line of his jaw and nose combined with a delicacy that rode a very fine edge between exotic strength and proud charm. His hair was thick, glossy black, a shade or two lighter than mine, and mostly straight save a few ends which curled up as if to protest the way every other hair on his head lay perfectly aligned.

A glimpse of his green eyes before the light had gone out in them was the same green as the peridot necklace my Omega father always used to wear. August-born, it was his birthstone, and my father loved stuff like that, giving meanings to things, and power, like gems and Zodiac signs and ancient symbols.

Kee wore nothing under a casual black vest, his broad chest rising and falling, gleaming bronze under the passing streetlights. His jeans gaped at the thighs, revealing smooth skin beneath. He smelled not of the streets, but of sugar cookies fresh from the oven, and peaches, and sunlight on new leaves, and something else I couldn't quite recall, something way back from childhood that both comforted and annoyed me.

Don't think.

None of it mattered. Kee was trouble. The end. Nothing good came of people like Kee, unless they changed from the

13

inside out. And when did that happen for people who were addicts and wild to the core? Never, probably. I saw it happen to my Omega brother who died at eighteen. I saw it all the time on the streets.

Life was the way it was, and stupid little shits like Kee got caught up in it and didn't even know what they were doing.

Whether Myre was right or wrong about Kee being a danger to his business, I was here, now, trying to hold him up, trying not to see the blood that ran from his nose and dripped from his upper lip where Stone had hit him hard.

Stupid boy. Silly child. I wanted to be done with this. Tonight. But knowing Myre, he'd prolong the drama of it all. He'd enjoy lording over his prisoner. He'd make him think there was hope that Omegas even affected him anymore at his age. He'd watch with sadistic pleasure as Kee used all his talents to get a reprieve, a pass, another chance. He'd make Kee think he was succeeding. And then, when Kee was most hopeful, eager to make any deal, he'd crush him. Squeeze him. Destroy him.

All because he thought Kee had a big mouth. Which perhaps he did, but not about this situation. But I couldn't say that to Myre. He wouldn't hear me.

I took a deep breath, letting it out slowly through flared nostrils.

Stone said, over the unconscious Omega, "Smells good, don't he?"

"Hadn't noticed." My voice sounded far away.

"Like hell you haven't."

Every muscle in my face hardened. I turned my head very slightly, and stared at him unblinking. It was one talent I possessed. Literature called it the *withering look*.

I didn't do chit-chat. Not with Stone, not with any of them. They disgusted me. All of them. I was only here for one thing. To get the job done.

Immediately, Stone glanced away.

Kee fell heavier against me as the car made a right turn. His long legs were spread, knees bent, his ass forward on the seat as he sprawled in slumber. His hair blended with my dark coat sleeve; the scent of him filled my nostrils—sweeter than most Omegas, with dark-edged addiction thrown in. It annoyed more than aroused. I'd had enough of prideful Omegas with pretty trappings. And the conceit of this one had gotten him trapped. Who could be amazed at that?

I might work for a man who had cornered the market on illegal narcotics in this sector, but I had no patience for addicts.

When we pulled into the parking garage of Diamond Edge, Myre's hotel and casino, Myre's driver came around and opened his door, escorting him ahead of us into his private entrance.

The shadows of the lower levels were shit-brown, the sodium lights piss-colored. I always felt like I stepped into a sewer here, though the garage was clean, and newly painted in all hues of gray. Down here, the air smelled of exhaust and car wash detergent and gasoline.

Stone came around to assist me with getting Kee from the backseat, but I didn't need his help. I pulled on Kee's calves until he slumped on his back, only his legs sticking out of the car. Then I reached inside and over his body, grabbing his arms and pulling him up against me. Lifting with my arms and straightening my back, I hefted him over my shoulder so his head hung at my spine and his legs flopped against my chest. Fireman's carry. He weighed more than he looked—all that muscle.

I spun easily, his weight distributed so I could maneuver with little effort, and followed the rest of them into Myre's personal elevator that would take us to the top floor where the private suites were.

The penthouse was Myre's, of course. The rest of the suites were usually empty. I stayed in one, gratis, on days when my hours went long, or when Myre had special assignments for me. Like today.

Myre once told me he liked me because I did as I was told without ever grumbling. While I didn't like Myre, or agree with many of his decisions about his business, I needed this job. I had my reasons.

In the small mirrored car, as we went up and up, no one spoke. Kee breathed heavily with a soft rasping sound, his head bumping me as the elevator slowed when it reached the top floor.

My arm around Kee's thighs, I stepped forward as the doors opened. The men let me exit with my burden first.

Myre said, in a clipped, rough tone, "Put him in the cage room."

I'd already guessed that was where I was headed. I'd spent some time there, watching the interrogators, slipping out when things turned serious. Of course I could kill when the need arose, for protection mostly. But I was a bodyguard, not an assassin. Myre had pros on the side for that sort of thing.

All the prisoners I'd babysat had been Alphas, threats to Myre's life or company. Ruthless. Murderers and rogues themselves. Or rats. Rarely did Myre take an Omega prisoner. They had no power. They were no threat.

Already I knew this was going to be different from the routine. I wasn't sure if Myre was planning on killing Kee. Alphas fighting among Alphas was one thing, even expected. But an Alpha taking on an Omega reeked of a special madness we'd been conditioned to fear since we were all kids. Our chemistry when mixed with an Omega's brought out protective instincts, or mating drives, more than anything else. Sure, Omegas might get hurt or even abused during Alpha Burns, but unless an Alpha was completely out of his mind, we treated Omegas as rather untouchable in that way.

Myre was running a business. He was more apt to see Omegas as commodities than enemies.

"Lock him up," Myre ordered me. "Keep watch. When he wakes, don't give him any food or water yet. Not until I send in Cyrus. And keep the lights low. I want him on edge for a while."

My eyebrows rose. It was going to be a long night. I'd already planned on getting no sleep.

I moved quickly down the hall toward the proper suite, pulling my keycard from my pocket with my free hand. I was one of the few Myre trusted enough to be given my own master key card. It opened any door at any hour.

I entered and set Kee down on the nearest couch, clean red leather polished to a shine. The cushions squeaked a bit under his weight.

I turned on the room's lights to see it was spotless, ready and waiting for Myre's next victim.

The room had been specially designed for Myre's brand of interrogations. The wall between the front room and bedroom had been removed. In its place was a line of metal bars and a barred door with a big lock.

It was all sparkling, the bars themselves like mirrors reflecting the overhead chandelier.

In the cage was a single bed against the wall, a toilet, a sink, and a tile floor with a drain in the center. The drain was put there as a psychological play. The hope was the prisoners would think it was there to catch the blood after they were killed. But Myre never soiled his own digs that way, including the cage room. He took his prisoners to other places for that final step.

An interrogation chair complete with straps, sat just outside the bars within easy sight of the room. Prisoners had to see it every time they woke or moved about the room. It teased and threatened the prisoners with what was to come.

An impeccable touch.

The couch was for me, mainly, or whoever was assigned babysitting duties. It faced away from the cell toward a flat screen TV on the wall. The TV was hooked into cable with every paid channel in existence, along with two different gaming devices.

17

Babysitters spent a lot of boring time here when prisoners were sleeping.

I glanced once at Kee, still unconscious, wasting his life by being both gorgeous and reckless at the same time, and turned to unlock the cage door.

Pushing it wide open, I went back to the couch, lifted Kee, this time in a cradle hold, and took him to the single bed, laying him carefully on it, making sure his legs were straight and his arms at his sides. I might have thought of him as a waste of a life, but it wasn't as if I wanted him to be uncomfortable.

His hair had become messed from me carrying him head down over my shoulder, and lay in tangles across his eyes and nose. I reached down to brush it back, but stopped, my hand an inch from his face.

What was I doing?

I reared back, dropping my hand quickly to my side as if I'd been burned. I looked him up and down, head to foot, his vest askew, his bare chest gleaming.

Hell, I could look at him all night and it wouldn't change a thing. Just because he was an Omega did not mean I would give him special treatment.

I left him sleeping and closed and locked the barred door. Then I went to the red leather couch, lay back upon it with my hands folded over my chest, and I waited.

Some time during the evening, my eyes closed.

Frantic yelling startled me awake.

"What the fuck! Let me outta here!"

Hands banging against metal. Shoes clomping against the hard tile flooring within the cage.

I opened my eyes, quickly orienting myself. I was in the cage suite. And yet another prisoner of Myre's was pissed.

I stared at the white-painted, beamed ceiling for about a minute before I bent my legs over the edge of the couch and sat up. I usually didn't fall asleep while babysitting, but it had been a long day. Myre had had me doing all sorts of meaningless tasks— from collecting money drops to following him around to his various meetings. Sometimes I forgot I was human and needed to eat and sleep.

"Hey, Alpha!" came the command from the cage. "Fucking let me outta here! You can't do this!"

I turned on the couch, placing both hands on the smooth, leather arm, and faced Kee. His face was damp from nerves, and he was practically throwing himself at the bars of the cage. His muscled body pushed and shoved against them, and his fists banged the hard metal.

There had to have been pain from his actions, but he didn't appear to feel it.

Our eyes met and Kee stood back for a second, his gaze boring into me. His eyes were green behind the dark hair flopping into his face, and he blew out a long breath. Aggressive for an Omega. Remarkable.

"Who the fuck are you?" Kee demanded.

I blinked slowly and lifted my chin. "Bast." We weren't supposed to give names in here. But when Myre wasn't around, I rather did as I pleased.

"Well, Bast," said Kee, "would you mind telling me what the fuck is going on?"

"What's going on," I replied in a low, calm voice, "is my boss wants to speak with you."

"And this is how he does business?"

"Sometimes." I drew out the single word in my low voice to see if it would get a reaction.

Kee continued to frown. "Are you like his assistant or something?"

"Or. Something."

"Well tell him to get in here and talk. So I can get this over with. I have appointments of my own, places I need to be."

His voice trailed off, going higher on the last word, a little shaky as if he knew his request, while quite reasonable, would never be met.

I turned away from him and faced the blank TV screen on the wall, thinking of turning it on. If I turned it up real loud, it might drown out his questions.

"Bast!"

I flicked my head toward him, eying him askance.

"Can't you tell me what's going on? Maybe we can make a deal?"

"Sorry. I can't." I spoke slowly, trying to project my nonchalance. Usually this sort of work didn't bother me too much, but this was an Omega. So he'd gotten a bit cocky and famous on the streets. So he talked a lot about dealers and deals. Who cared?

Except he had cops for clients, and two of Myre's best had just been arrested. Someone had to go down for it. For days, Myre kept saying, "That filthy street Omega everyone talks about, he's too loose with his money and drugs. He's too loose-lipped and hangs with pigs."

It wasn't good to be loose-lipped in our work, but Kee didn't work for us. Still, Myre had something against the guy, and now here he was.

Kee banged his palm hard against one bar, and swore. Out the corner of my eye, he spun and hugged his hand to his chest. His jeans hugged tight at his hips, tugging against the two rips high on the backs of his thighs. The bare skin pressed against the material, smooth and hard, meant to draw the eye.

I glanced away. I'd held the guy over my shoulder. I'd felt his heat, his weight, and the firmness of his muscles on the backs of his legs. I'd already touched that skin—on his arms and chest—and knew it to be silken. But seeing those cuts in the jeans fabric made him seem suddenly vulnerable. Or cute. Or something I couldn't allow my mind to focus on.

I made a deep sound, low in my throat. If I'd been an animal it would have been a growl. Well, maybe it still was a growl. It managed to intimidate a lot of people, but mainly it was a habitual reaction for when I was annoyed, miserable, or unhappy. It wasn't about anyone but me. My own personal criticism of my current life.

More grumbles from the cell.

"Am I supposed to use this toilet? Really? Without any privacy? And there's no food. Is food being brought at any time soon? What about water? Am I to drink from the sink?"

I said nothing.

"Who the fuck does this anyway? Puts someone in a cage like this? I haven't done anything! I don't owe anyone a thing! What? Does he have a kink or something for this? Is your boss wanting to fuck me in a prison cell? Is that it?"

"Yes. Well. We'll just wait and see, won't we?" When I spoke, I didn't look at him. But I saw movement, Kee beginning to pace the length of his confinement.

"Wait? How long?" His breaths came out like hisses.

I reached out to the end table and grabbed the remote, turning on the TV. I didn't care what came on, just as long as it was noise.

Kee paced. He kept calling out to me.

"Hey!"

"Bast!"

I ignored him.

After a while I got up and glanced at the clock over the stove. I noted two hours had passed since I'd brought Kee here. Had I napped that long?

After a while, I got up and went to the fridge at the far end of the suite, out of sight of Kee. I didn't drink on duty, so ignored the cold beers in favor of a sugared cola.

The fridge was well-stocked with drinks and sandwich makings.

Myre had been clear that I wasn't to give Kee food or water. But he had to be thirsty. All the drinks he'd had served to him, gifts from various bar customers looking to get lucky, had to have taken a toll. And he'd had drugs in his pockets, which Stone had emptied in the alley trash before we'd wrestled him into the car. I wasn't sure he was on anything right now, but if he was coming down, it might be uncomfortable.

Well, Myre had said no water. He hadn't said no soda.

I grabbed a plastic cup from the cupboard, took another cola from the fridge and poured it into the cup.

When I came into the main room with the drinks and saw Kee looking at me, then glancing at the drinks in my hand, I realized I was letting empathy intrude with my job.

Yes, I had empathy. But on the job I tried to curb it.

Kee licked his lips. "I'm thirsty." He flattened his lips and glared.

I stopped about six feet away from the bars.

"If you were truly thirsty, you could do as you suggested earlier and drink from the sink faucet."

He turned his head away from me, rolling his eyes. "I wouldn't have to do that if you'd just let me out of here."

"No."

"If your boss wants a word with me, I'll cooperate. Like normal. We sit face to face and we talk."

That would never happen. Myre was a paranoid fuck.

I closed my eyes, then opened them slowly, suppressing a sigh.

"Bast, I swear it. Why the drama of the cage? I'm not a danger. If your boss wants to talk to me so bad, then he knows that."

I was used to this. First, the prey tries to reason his way out, pretend he's a cooperative captive.

"You look pretty smart," Kee continued. "So you know I'm telling the truth. I'm just an Omega, nobody, really. Come on. We'll wait together. I hear your TV. We can just watch a movie and wait."

"Do you," I began, very slowly. Then stopped and started again. I used this tactic partly because I was bored, but also because I knew if I spoke slowly so they hung on every word, it got their attention as well as intimidated them.

"Do you want this cola or not?"

22

"Is it drugged? Is it going to make me sick?"

"I don't know. Are you allergic to soda?"

"No. But why should I trust you?"

"Very well." I started to turn away.

"No! No! I want it. I do. I do!"

"If I give it to you, will you shut up, then?"

Kee's smooth eyebrows shot downward, as if pain lanced his forehead. He probably did have a headache after the punch Stone had given him. A trace of blood still edged the right side of his mouth. He'd managed to wipe the rest away. The caffeine would do him good, not that I cared.

As if not hearing—or understanding my words—Kee said, "I swear, I'll be good. I'll give *you* a good time, if you just let me out. Please!"

In one of the drawers in the kitchen, I kept earplugs for situations like these. I contemplated setting down both drinks and getting them.

Kee blurted out quickly, "Okay, I'll be quiet. I swear. I'll take the drink."

If it would shut him up, I'd do almost anything.

But of course, I didn't believe him. It didn't matter. I'd always intended to give him the drink.

I walked to the edge of the cage and stuck my hand out as far as the bars. Kee had to thrust his hand out and lean against the bars to reach me. He scowled as he took the plastic glass and looked down.

"What, no ice?"

I almost knocked it out of his hand, then. I would have been able to. He hadn't backed up and I could easily reach him.

Instead, I turned my back on him and went back to the red leather couch, taking a drag of my cola from the bottle, which I preferred. The taste was better when it came from the original glass bottle it was packaged in. Sweet with a punch, and cold.

I sat facing away from Kee, and put my legs up on a low, square coffee table in front of the couch. I'd worn my ankle boots today, black leather with a silver button on the outside of each, and I crossed my ankles and wiggled my toes within them. I would have preferred taking them off, but if Myre came in and I was in stocking feet, I'd feel completely wrong. Unfinished. Not to the job.

As it was, I remained unwrinkled and in order. My nap had not messed anything up. My hair was still combed straight back in a gleaming cap, set behind my ears. With the right cut and comb, and a bit of mousse, it stayed where I wanted it.

I heard scuffling from the cage. Heavy sighing. A whimper.

I shut my eyes and counted to ten, then opened them. The TV blared some romantic scene. The Alpha and Omega couple on the screen were making love. Badly. No chemistry. All arms and legs getting in the way of things, though the Omega did have a cute ass.

A voice wafted over the sounds of kissing and moaning.

"I think I've seen that one," said Kee. "I can only hear it, but it's a terrible movie. Just sayin'."

I ignored him.

"I think the Omega ends up killing his lover because the Alpha is, well, as they say, unable to keep his dick in his pants. There's a murder trial. It's really awful. You should change the channel."

"Don't talk." I spoke in an ordinary tone, staring forward, seeing nothing.

Blessed silence filled the room. For about two minutes.

"Your people seem, well, kinda serious."

I predicted the next question. They all asked it. It was part of the endless routine.

"Why am I here? Do you think they'll kill me or something?" Kee's voice went higher on that last word.

It didn't look good for him. Myre was not the type to go soft on the enemy of the day. He had a paranoid streak. And a lot of power. He was never soft about plowing over those he perceived to be in his way regarding his business.

24

"Bast? You're not answering. That means yes. He will kill me. Right?"

"I do not make those decisions," I replied, glancing toward the cage.

"But you work for him. You know." A hitch to the tone now, a bitter edge.

I reached for the remote to turn the sound on the TV up.

"What did I do?" Kee asked. "I'm a harmless guy. I may party a bit hard, but I don't hurt others. Never."

Right. He could put that in his last confession. Many times Myre gave guys a chance at last words before his assassins pulled the trigger. The times he had me do it, I didn't prolong it.

I started flipping through channels before I found some sports highlights. I didn't follow any particular sport or team, but this would distract for a time.

I heard the suite's door lock click with someone's key-card, then open. Immediately, I stood, moving away from the couch and lowering the volume on the TV.

Myre walked in, followed by Stone and another man named Merch. I never liked Merch. He wore a permanent half smirk, half smile no matter what was going on around him. He liked to kick those who were down.

"How's our little Omega?" Myre asked, barely glancing at the cage.

The Omega was far from little, but I wasn't going to argue that detail.

Kee took a step back, his face going pale.

"He give you any trouble?" Myre's dark suit was so finely pressed the creases in front of the ankles looked sharp as blades. He'd removed his tie since we'd gone out, but otherwise, he appeared slick as ever.

Slowly, I turned my head toward Kee. The plastic cup I'd given him earlier was sitting on the edge of the sink in full view. Myre had to see it, but he said nothing.

"No, sir," I replied.

Kee met my gaze, the muscles around his eyes drawn, his mouth open to just a slit, posture frozen.

Myre gestured with one hand to Stone. He didn't have to say anything. Stone went to the cage and opened the door with a card. It swung outward, and Kee backed up a step, eyes moving from me to Stone and back to me.

"Thank you for your assistance, Bast," said Myre.

This was my moment, my cue to exit.

Why I hesitated, I didn't know. But some inner part of me fluttered aware, like a door opening, but to what I couldn't tell. I opened my mouth. One word forced its way out. "I."

Myre looked at me, eyebrows angled. "I—what?"

I shook my head.

"That will be all for tonight," Myre said to me. "Get a few hours sleep. I may have need of you later."

"Yes, sir." That meant I'd stay in one of the guest suites so I'd be nearby. On call. A room had already been designated for me long ago.

But it felt wrong. Leaving. Staying. Keeping an Omega on ice as if he were someone dangerous. He wasn't. Not at all. But Myre had become obsessed.

I had a few phone calls to make, but not here. I never did any personal business here. Everything was monitored and I hated it. If I tried to slip away tonight, others would notice.

I could do nothing but walk to the door, step into the hall, and close it behind me.

Chills ran up and down my arms and legs. My spine. This wasn't like me. But then again, too much of what I did these days had little to do with me, and more to do with feeling about as trapped as the *little* Omega in Myre's grasp.

Chapter Three

Kee

The second he walked in, I recognized the guy from Moosie's bar. The guy who looked like he'd spent years in the desert. The guy who wore a silk-wool blend like it was a second skin and flashed diamonds on his pinkies. He'd been staring at me while I'd sat with my friends, and still stood there by a table at the front when I'd left for the bathroom to buy some fun. The one Tobi had called Myre.

His dark eyes held a hunger I didn't recognize, shielded by decades-old ice. He'd wanted me, and now he had me. But not for reasons most Alphas wanted Omegas.

A shudder ran through me as the one Myre had called Stone grabbed me hard by the arm and yanked me through the cage entrance, half-dragging me to the chair with the straps.

I made no sound, my voice frozen in my throat. The edges of my vision went dark for a moment. I licked at my cut lip, the skin stinging.

While Stone fastened straps to my wrists and ankles, the other two Alphas stood over me, tall and dark shadowed, invading my personal space. One of them laid out a cloth with metal instruments on it on a little side table. Weapons, I guessed. Like knives, and metal batons, and stuff I couldn't quite see, but it all glittered under the ivory light from a stupid crystal chandelier overhead.

This place was posh, but they'd made a cage out of it, and a torture room. Who did that?

Would they kill me? When I'd asked Bast the question, he'd never answered. He'd never responded to most of my questions.

I kept my head down, my eyes half-closed. Shudders wracked me within, but I clenched my fists to keep from showing my outright fear. I didn't scare easily.

I took on any Alpha who came crossed my path with money in his fist because that was my way. I knew I could easily seduce them. I didn't mind it rough. But this—this was new to me. Sure, I'd had Alphas smack me around a bit, but I'd always persevered. Maybe I'd just been lucky.

My usual self would come up cocky, smiling and chatty, wide open for any compromise. But I didn't have to be psychic to know these guys weren't going to be open for a quick fuck and then letting me go.

Questions stormed my brain. I had a million of them. But they looked like they were going to be doing the questioning. I sat very still. If it made me look guilty—though I'd done nothing—I had no control over that.

One of them, Stone I think, spoke from just inside the cell. "Bast's been up to some tricks. Fuck, he's being nice to this guy or something?"

I had no idea what he meant, but then I saw a plastic cup go flying. My soda cup. Now I could truly see that Bast was different from the others. This one called Stone never would have given me a cup of soda. That drink had been a kind reprieve. I still tasted the sugar on the sides of my tongue.

A muscle in old wrinkly face's cheek twitched as that side of his mouth quirked up. Myre said, "And you would have him punished."

Stone came out and put his hands on his hips. "Simply pointing out he refuses to comply one hundred percent."

"My orders. My worry."

I saw only their bodies from the chest down. I refused to lift my eyes any further.

"Just give me the word and I'll have him back at a hundred percent," snarled Stone.

Myre let out a low, short chuckle, devoid of mirth. "You see one side. Bast sees two. Who do you think has the better perspective when it comes to my well-being?"

Stone's body froze, then backed up half a step.

So, Bast was held in high esteem, it seemed, in Myre's mind.

A hand came toward my face so fast I flinched. Fingers went under my chin and tilted my head up. Myre glared at me with his dark-as-space eyes only inches away. Hot breath wafted against my forehead.

"What do you think, Omega slut?"

"I—I--" My throat closed up. I'd been in denial about the reality of this situation for hours. Now my body caught up. My internal shivers came on strong, blocking my breaths as well as my voice.

"Did Bast harm you in any way?"

"N—no."

"See?" He turned to Stone. "I can't say I would have trusted you to do the same."

Stone scowled, and let out a breath that puffed his cheeks. His eyes glittered yet at the same time seemed devoid of light.

"My name is Myre. If you haven't heard of me, then I've done my job. Invisibility is my talent. But now it's time for you to know I run the streets here, and the more profitable portions of this ungodly city. Why do you think I'm telling you this now?"

I gulped twice. "I—I don't know."

"Because after tonight, I know you can be trusted with that information."

Was he trying to scare me? Blackmail me? Hire me to scrape the gutter dirt off the bottoms of his shoes?

"But first," Myre continued. "Before we deal with that. I need you to give me some rules. It's very simple. I ask you a question. You answer honestly. I am excellent at detecting a lie. If you lie, I order Merch here to start breaking bones. First the little ones like a finger or a toe. Did you know the penis has a bone that can be very painful when it breaks?"

I nodded once, holding my breath. I certainly didn't want him to break my junk.

"We have an understanding?"

My heart slammed my chest. Questions about what? What did I know that this Alpha would be interested in? I tried not to squirm. The room fogged up a bit as cold tears prickled my vision. I could only nod.

"All right, then. Now you know the rules and we can begin."

Myre's first questions were about my dealers. He wanted their names. First and last. I nearly panicked when I told him I did not know their last names. Would he believe me?

But so far, all my toes and fingers—and my cock— remained intact.

Next, he wanted to know about some of my clients. Namely, the cops who hired me to see them through their Burns.

As I gave their names, a sense of betrayal scraped along the bottom of my stomach. I didn't name drop client to client. Sometimes we Omegas talked amongst ourselves, but in whispers. In alcoves where voices never carried. Who was dangerous on the path this week? What were the trends for Omegas being hurt or never being seen or heard from again?

The good cops actually looked out for us. I hated outing them. But I couldn't ignore the surly guy standing next to me holding a set of pliers that promised agony in places I didn't want to think about.

Myre gave me two names. First and last. He said them slowly. Carefully, leaning down to look closer into my eyes.

"Do you know them?" he asked.

I shook my head.

"Think very carefully."

"Honestly, I don't. Who are they? Alphas? Omegas?"

"Boss," interrupted Stone.

Myre spun and snapped out. "What is it?"

"They go by street names."

Myre straightened. "And they are?"

"Dill. And Guff."

"I do know them," I blurted.

Myre turned back to me. "How?"

"They—they're Alphas. They are always together. They go to a lot of parties. You know the kind where Alphas pay and share the Omegas around. It's—it can be rough—go all night. But they pay well."

Pliers clicked at my ear. Myre was getting antsy. Wanting blood. Some Alphas just didn't know when to keep it in their pants.

"How well did you know them?" Myre asked.

"Not well at all. Just in passing. Names. Faces. They repeat. The same people come and go in the Trenches in phases."

"Did they ever pay for your services?"

They had. Both of them. And they also talked a lot as they fucked me together—as if having a threesome was as boring an activity as eating or sleeping. They dropped names I didn't know and some I did know. They were full of larger than life secrets and I admit I paid attention. They joked and they always had a lot of drugs to spread around—steam, mainly. They were rich. They bragged about everything, including wealth. They were gamblers who hit a lot of jackpots at the casino.

My face went white.

"Yes." I held my breath, waiting.

"I see."

"They—they weren't friends or anything," I offered.

"Well, of course not. You wouldn't sell out your friends to your cop lovers, now, would you?"

Stunned, I tensed so hard the chair rocked. "Sell out?"

"Don't pretend to be surprised. They were arrested two days ago. One is my beloved cousin I've known since childhood. The other a good family friend."

"Arrested? I don't know anything about--"

"Your reputation is you get around. You have a big mouth. You talk the big talk like you're somebody—somebody more than the street scum Omega slut you are. I have spies everywhere. I see with more than just my eyes."

I clamped my teeth together to keep my jaw from shaking.

"Kee has notoriety on the streets. Others come to Kee, look up to Kee. If they need something, Kee can get it or tell them where to get it."

It did not appear to bode well for me that Myre had started referring to me in the third person as if I weren't even here.

"I think you're smarter than you let on," Myre said. "I think you listen to and remember every word out of your clients' mouths, and for the right price, you can provide information to anyone. You're an unbonded Omega. You obviously have no loyalties."

"I don't sell information to anyone!" It was the first lie I'd told during this interrogation. Truth was, I'd do anything for money. And had. And Dill and Guff talked a lot. But no one had ever asked me about them specifically.

A hand clamped down on my wrist. Thick, cold metal touched my pinky finger and the teeth on the insides of the pliers' mouth dug into my first knuckle.

"When your cop friends came around asking questions, offering you money, sticking their tiny dicks into you to make you cry for more, you spilled anything they wanted to know. They let you go every time. Why? You're a little infant, sucking at the teat of a drug empire for your cheap highs, buying and maybe even selling steam on my turf, right under their noses. I have your file. You've never been arrested. Why is that?"

My words croaked out. "Cops do steam, too. You know that. Half the force is corrupt."

"Yes, and that half works for me. Which is how I know you have such a big mouth. How I know you've been selling information to them."

Myre nodded his head in the direction of the Alpha he'd called Merch who had his hands on me.

I knew it was happening before it happened. I opened my mouth and let out a strange scream, a sound I'd never heard come from my own throat before.

The click and the pain in my little finger came seconds later, when it was all over. Warmth flooded my whole hand as endorphins kicked in, but it wasn't enough. The pain nearly made me pass out.

Through my dizziness, I glanced down. My finger was red with blood. He'd cut through the skin. The little finger of my right hand looked flattened at the first knuckle. When I tried to move it, pain like a knife shot through it and into my hand and wrist.

"Now," said Myre. "Tell me everything you told the cops."

My scream still echoed in the room. I could hear it over and over in my mind. My breaths came in gushing, quick puffs. Tears rolled like lava down my cheeks.

I wanted to scream again, to beg them to let me go. I wanted to make promises it was too late to make. Offer myself. Give them anything they wanted. If only they'd let me walk out of this room. If only they would let me live.

I couldn't believe this was happening to me. At twenty-five my life had come to this. I always knew deep inside me I would probably not live to be thirty. Some instinct informed me of this as if it were a fact, which was why I partied hard and made no commitments, formed no loyalties, but I didn't think I'd be cut off so soon. Not in this manner.

I looked up at Myre, my lashes sticky as I blinked. "I'll tell you everything."

"Just as I thought," Myre replied with a stark smile. "No honor."

Chapter Four

Bast

The bed was a state of the art classic king, the most expensive on the market with a topper to die for, clean soft sheets, pillows made of part foam, part cloud. The room temperature was perfect. The silence stretched like paradise forever, my number one favorite tune.

I could not deny I had extended luxuries in this job. And bliss when I needed it.

But I couldn't sleep.

I needed to make a phone call that could not be done here. I needed to slip out and back without anyone seeing me. It was bothering me that I felt trapped, walled in, no better than that beguiling Omega just down the hall.

Kee. His face imploring as I left the prison suite. More vulnerable-looking than he probably knew. Those guys of Myre's would eat him alive, not to mention the boss himself who had a deep appetite for control, a dominant mastery that not only bordered on obsessive, but downright owned the term.

I got up and put on yesterday's suit sans blazer, opting for my favorite long, light-weight coat. I loved the coat; it made me feel cloaked, hidden, but intimidating to those who dealt with me.

In the hall, bathed twenty-four/seven in golden light, Spiro, one of Myre's night guards, stood by the elevators looking bored. He glanced up at my approach, the long scar down the side of his cheek looking red tonight, as if he'd been scratching at it.

I held out my key-card.

Spiro frowned. "Boss said no one is to enter or leave this floor tonight."

"Who do you think you're talking to?" I said it low, trying to keep my voice non-threatening. It was difficult at the best of times. I tried to tell myself for years now that people didn't *try* to be annoying. They simply were.

"I know but." Spiro swallowed.

"I outrank you."

The face-off lasted less than three seconds. Spiro moved to the side, and his brown hair fell onto his monstrously high forehead making him even more annoying. And flustered.

"What should I say if I'm asked?"

"About what?" I started to turn my back on him.

"Where you're going?"

"To the corner for a pack of smokes." I didn't smoke. But no one here knew that. I pretended to. I lit the cigarettes and filled ashtrays with their butts. They never touched my lips.

"Yeah, uh." He winced a bit. "Okay."

"I'll be back before anyone notices."

He made a strange grunt, then said, "See ya."

Idiot.

I knew where all the cameras were in the casino and elsewhere. Myre had had me inspect them. I'd gone over security footage from many of them as my job for Myre included finding people, tracking people. I knew all the dead zones, all the places not tracked by security as a rule but only there for back up.

It was easy to make my path untraceable.

Once outside, I knew which CCTV cameras to avoid and I easily blended with the shadows. The next block up stood the empty building Myre had bought as a tax write-off. Small. Three stories. All offices scattered with leftover filing cabinets, some on their sides, rooms with peeling paint and acoustic ceilings stained yellow and, in some places, completely broken away.

No one came here. Ever. I had all the keys. But just in case anyone broke in, I had put what I needed now on the top floor in the far bathroom. That room had flooded and still had sewage dried all over the floor and looked too scary of a place for even the most desperate drunken teen or homeless desperado to enter.

I flashed my pin-light ahead of me to show my path. The stairwells were open and clear as I made my way to the third floor. I was happy to get to the bathroom without being accosted by a single rat.

The toilet tank in the corner cubicle had long since dried, but I kept my stuff in a plastic bag just in case the water came back on for some unknown reason. Just in case.

Lifting the lid, I took out the bag and walked into the office next door where there was still a viable desk chair with a stained cushion, useful to no one but ghosts—and me—and sat, pin-light in my mouth, to go through my things.

I set the black billfold containing petty cash of a few grand aside. I had a keychain with a little yellow plastic fawn on it with big eyelashes painted around its eyes. Completely innocuous as a child's toy if ever found, but it contained a key to a storage shed on the far side of the city where I kept a few boxes of personal items from my past, as well as the first car I'd ever owned that was no longer running: a black Cobra Mustang.

Setting that aside, I brought out a flat silk bag with a drawstring on top. I untied it and slipped the cell phone into my palm. It was an old style phone with a flip screen.

From my pocket, I brought out my portable charger and plug, and attached it to the phone. Immediately, it lit up. I took the pin-light out of my mouth and set it on the floor. Then, I tapped in a number I knew by heart.

A voice on the other end said, "Hey."

"A heads up about Dill and Guff would have been nice," I said.

"You're impossible to contact."

"Myre's brought in a street Omega to torture and blame for the arrests."

"Yeah, well."

"Well? That's all you have to say?" I asked.

Sam, my contact on the force never went into the field, so it was hard for him to understand that real people were involved in his decisions, and not simply names and statistics.

I huffed into the phone. "He's innocent. Sure, the Omega talks a lot, but I'm the one who gave you the tip and the evidence on those two trouble-makers. You're responsible for that Omega's life now."

"What? What do you care about a silly street Omega? This is bigger than all that, and you know, after all these years, there're always casualties."

"Yeah. Acceptable losses. Only, he's friendly with some of your staff and he's going to give Myre their names if he hasn't already."

"You told me yourself, Myre doesn't kill cops. Brings on too much heat. If there's a more imminent danger, contact us then."

"That's it? You're not going to do anything?"

"What's the Omega's name?" Sam asked.

"Kee. I don't know his last name."

"I'll make sure a memo goes out that no one is to deal with a boy named Kee ever again."

"You won't have to write that memo. He'll be dead before it's read."

A pause. A bit of soft breathing. "Problem solved," came the slow response.

"You're a dick, you know that." It was not a question.

"What would you have me do that doesn't put you or this operation in jeopardy of being discovered?" Sam asked.

"I'll think on it."

"Oh no you don't. Bast, you're not going to do a thing. Don't say anything. Don't do anything. Don't lift a finger. You'll compromise everything."

"Yeah."

"I mean it. That's an order, Sebastian."

When I did not reply, Sam said, "You heard me, right?"

I stared at the phone.

"Have I made myself clear?" Sam asked.

"Crystal." I put as much venom into that one word as I could muster, then flipped the phone closed effectively cutting off my handler.

I put everything back in the plastic bag, sealed it, and put it back in the tank of the toilet.

By the time I got back to the casino and the top floor, not even a half an hour had passed. I stopped by the corner market and bought two packs of cigs.

When I came out of the elevator, I handed one pack to Spiro. The brand was his favorite.

"Hey, thanks."

"Going back to bed now," I mumbled.

Chapter Five

Kee

Seriously, the guy must have spent too long in the desert. Myre's wrinkles were too many to count. His brain appeared fried. He asked me questions that made no sense. Stuff about evidence the cops had on his beloved cousin and friend. Stuff about their activities I'd never heard of before, not from their lips while they fucked me, or anyone else's.

"It wasn't me."

How many times had I said those words? Dozens. How many times did they make no difference? More dozens.

It seemed to go on for hours. When the jerk with the pliers squeezed my middle toe, I peed myself. None of them seemed to care, like they saw it every day—guys begging for relief, guys crying and denying, guys emptying their bladders in pain and fear.

I wasn't ignorant. I knew there was a system in place on the streets for drug supplies and other harsher stuff, but I steered clear of it. It was only the steam I liked a little too much. If I sold any extra steam I had, it was only to friends. I bought mainly at clubs or bars, not in the open in the Trenches.

After the questioning became more detailed and furious, Myre wasn't buying my answers. He kept at it, though, for what seemed like hours, though it was still night. I could see the shadows behind the floor-to-ceiling curtains on the wall that faced the cage, and they were darker than dawn or pre-dawn. The middle of the night had never lasted so long.

I couldn't speak anymore. I couldn't think. I was dizzy and sticky and bloody on my toe, and my split lip had started to bleed again.

Someone was undoing the straps at my wrists. My legs were already free, my bare feet dragging the floor as I was yanked up and out of the chair.

The last few minutes were a blur. Had I passed out?

"Clean him up." Myre's voice came as if from far away. "Let him rest and then get him ready for a drive. Dawn."

The hands that held me tossed me to the floor of the cell and I hit my sore hand and scraped my knees through my now even more ripped up blue jeans. I couldn't move, see or think.

Hands with a rough, wet towel washed my face, hands and feet. The towel met my blurry vision, spotted red.

"Please," I said. "I don't know anything." My words fell on dead air. The cell door banged shut.

I crawled on my knees and one good hand to the cot, and curled up on the thin mattress, strange lights and images swirling through my mind. My throat was so dry it hurt to breathe. It seemed like eons had passed since Bast had given me the soda in a plastic cup.

My damp jeans pulled at the crotch, the smell sour agonizing combined with everything else. This was it. I'd reached the end of my path. I hoped it would be quick, then began to sob at the thought. Quick, hoarse sounds that wrenched my already sore body.

My broken finger had gone numb; my toe throbbed with fierce stabs.

My last thought as I lost consciousness for a bit was: *That old man Alpha—it wasn't the desert he'd come from; it was Hell.*

*

When I woke, I could not ascertain time at all. Had I slept minutes or hours?

I rolled onto my back, forgetting for a moment where I was. The pain hit me full force and my muscles went taut, my legs and arms stiffening. I cried out.

40

Voices came from the other side of the suite, outside the bars of my cage. They must have been what woke me.

I did not want to open my eyes. I didn't want to see the metal bars or the red couch, or the marble topped kitchen counters. I didn't want to see the long curtains in case they were lighter, in case dawn approached.

The door to my cell clanged loudly as it swung open, the hinges making a slow reverberating moan. Hands grabbed my upper arm, tugging.

"Up, Omega!"

I tried to turn away, but whoever it was was too strong. I nearly fell as my body was yanked to the edge of the bed. I got my feet under me, gasping in pain from my toe, holding my sore hand close to my chest. My usually perfect hair hung in tangled strands, tickling my face.

With one guy holding me up on the side, I limped forward, unseeing.

Dawn had arrived. Next would come the drive. Myre's parting words chilled me to the core. They weren't taking me to a viewpoint to watch the sunrise, that I knew for sure.

"Well that's just perfect now, isn't it? He can't even walk." A voice hissed the words. It sounded like Bast.

"Who cares?" said another. "It's private elevators all the way down."

"People get lost. People wander where they're not supposed to be. If he's seen--"

"They'll just think he's another drunk fuck. An Omega hired for an all-nighter."

"Right." The sound of Bast's voice was flat and firm. Truly pissed.

I wanted to smile because he'd been the only guy who'd showed me any true kindness even if it was behind a glacier façade. Where was he in the room? I couldn't see. Maybe I could look into his face as I died and it wouldn't be so awful. He'd given me the soda against the boss's orders. I'd argue to my last breath that at least some part of him cared. If anyone cared that

I died, it would be one more than existed less than twelve hours ago, for I had no true and real friends, not even Tarin, one of my repeat Alpha customers who'd tried so hard to tame me, who thought he even loved me. I'd laughed in his face too many times to count.

Now, I wished I was with him in the posh guest room he'd always set aside for me, letting him cook for me, letting him fuck me through his Burns. He'd told me he wanted a bond with me.

I'd felt no spark of it on my end. Besides, we were opposites in too many ways. I was no good for him. I'd never be what he wanted, so I'd laughed at that, too, and left him over and over. Poor Tarin, always so worried for the little Omegas who had no homes or high educations, the Omegas who had no rights in his Alpha-ruled world.

But even now as I thought of Tarin, my heart cracked wide open, and a pain lanced my chest with needle precision. What a stupid boy I'd been. Thankless at best, rude and condescending in my worst states.

Alphas, for the most part, infuriated me. I bent over and I took their money, but as for my feelings for them? They fueled my hate for the world, and for my life.

Steam took care of my anxieties, and fucking. Add alcohol to the mix and I lost days at a time. The rare times I was sober, I worked out hard to kick up the endorphins. Being high was my medicine for the disease called life.

Yeah, Tarin was a fool, but a nice fool. If I'd simply stayed on with him, letting him take care of me, I wouldn't be here now facing the dawn.

I stumbled from the cage and blinked to steady my vision, a black form in front of me coalescing into Bast.

Strong arms caught me. My good hand brushed his side, the dark shirt beneath my palm silken, warm. He smelled of soap, clean and windswept, but with something bitter-burnt beneath, like pain, like a strictness I needed, like someone who might stay me with a look and a firm hand. Someone who might not be afraid to tell me the truth, that I was a lost, lost boy who'd fucked up real bad.

It was too late for all that now.

But hell, if I was dying, I could fantasize about Bast if I wanted. Hey, I got a pass.

"Steady now," came the low, almost too-deep voice.

I closed my eyes and breathed in.

"You got him?" said another voice. It sounded like Stone.

"Yep. I got him." Bast sounded all too bored, but with my head against his chest, I felt his heart thrumming fast and high-strung.

The Alpha's head leaned toward mine and he said into my ear, "Come along."

I limped, then stumbled again.

"Up." Bast held me up with both hands.

"I can't," I whispered.

"You can. You will."

Following his lead, I made a few more steps before he cursed under his breath and picked me up like a child, one arm under my knees, one under my shoulders.

I leaned into his chest even further and clutched my good hand at his satiny shirt, not caring if I wrinkled or tore it. My other hand with the broken finger I pressed hard to my own chest, trying not to jar it.

We exited the suite and entered a hall. I could see the high ceiling and the inlaid, golden lights and the edges of the narrowed walls.

I heard someone speak but could not make out the words. Then an elevator dinged.

It was ridiculous. I clung to the guy who was carrying me off to kill me. I knew it in my gut. My brain was freaking out. But I couldn't move, and with every step he took, I pressed myself tighter against him, clinging literally for my life.

What kind of person clung to their murderer? But he was all I had. I was losing, loser, lost. Drifting already toward the unknown.

The elevator went a long way down. From my vantage, I could see the numbers up high, going from twelve to negative two. Down below. Maybe to some parking garage? I didn't know. I'd been unconscious when I was brought here.

When the elevator arrived, we exited, and the footfalls of the Alphas echoed eerily through the shadows of—yes, I'd guessed correctly—the parking garage.

"He's really out of it. Did you give him something?" Bast's voice rumbled from his chest and straight into my ear.

"Nothing," came the response.

I heard an engine running, smelled gas fumes and the oily scent of many cars. A car door opened. I turned my head and saw a black sedan and an Alpha who looked like a chauffeur standing by the backseat entrance.

The car looked new, sleek and long. Okay, so we had a driver. For some reason that gave me heart. If there was a third party involved, wouldn't that be too many witnesses? Maybe they weren't going to kill me after all. Maybe they were taking me to a doctor.

Yeah. I was so deluded I'd grasp a belief in any fantasy at this point.

Bast bent down and put me on my bare feet. "In," he ordered.

I practically fell back onto the seat, managing to lift my legs and swing them inside. My hair slapped me in the eyes, stinging, and I reached up to wipe it away. My hand came away wet with tears.

I started to open my mouth, to beg, and shut it. What good would it do? I'd given up. I had no more choices left anyway, no more branches on my path.

The driver got in and revved the engine. We took off. The tires gave soft little screams on the concrete.

I started to shake harder. "One way trip," I said in a shaky voice.

The Alpha named Stone was on my other side. "Shut up," he snapped.

Bast took a breath and let it out hard.

Myre did not come with us. I supposed he gave orders to kill but left the dirty work to his underlings. It made sense.

I wanted to say so many things. I wanted to plead, to convince, to make them feel sorry for me. But my voice stopped every time I opened my mouth. My body felt cold already, my own will too distant to reach. All parts of me ached. It would be a relief, I told myself, to sleep forever.

No orders were given to the driver as to our destination. It had all been planned ahead.

Beside me, Bast sat ramrod straight, facing directly ahead. I turned to watch him—he was so controlled, so still— and he did not seem to notice I was there at all. He behaved as if in a trance. His eyes did not blink. The lights from outside on the streets flashing in his hair were the only movements about him. In the window's reflection, he could have been a life-sized doll.

I wanted him to touch me. Hold me when I died. Would he if I asked? No. I thought not. It would be too much to expect. Especially from a stranger of his lot, mixed up with organized crime, the worst of the lot of criminals I'd encountered.

After driving for about fifteen minutes on the highway, the car went up some side streets and into the hills where there was little light and only an occasional signpost naming yet more side roads. Quail Avenue. Rose Lane. Star Court.

The trees grew taller, the underbrush thicker.

We turned off onto a dirt road, drove another mile over hard packed, ridged dirt. Stone shifted and cursed beside me. Bast remained unaffected.

When the car stopped, I saw only trees and the deeper darknesses within the forest. The sky was slate now, but the sun still missing.

"Get out," Stone ordered. To who? All of us?

"No." Bast finally spoke.

"What?" Stone turned to look at him, leaning hard into me. I shut my eyes.

"I'll do it." Bast shifted beside me.

"Fuck. I don't give a shit. You wanna? I'll just sit back and have my morning smoke."

"Yes. I want to."

Bast got out, then helped me out behind him. He left me standing, leaning, actually, against the back of the car as he opened the trunk. He brought out a brand new package of plastic sheeting. And a shovel.

When he closed the trunk, he looked at me with emotionless, black eyes. "You're not going to give me trouble, all right?"

I burst into tears.

He ignored me, and grabbed my arm with his free hand, and steered me under the trees. There was no path, just lots of wild foliage and weeds underfoot. The birds had been singing in the pre-sunrise, but they stopped as our footfalls crashed against leaves and branches.

Barefoot, I tripped a lot, nearly falling, but Bast held me up. We walked away from the car for about ten minutes. Then he stopped.

We were in a sort of clearing near some tall, thick-trunked pines. Bast looked around, sniffing the air, which was fresh and clean, the sharp pine fragrance reminding me of childhood when I was very young, when I still had my Omega father. Old winter holidays I'd never see again flashed back to me.

"Sit," Bast ordered.

I glanced about. All was dirt, dead leaves, and weeds. "Where?" The word stumbled from my mouth. I was still crying.

He pointed to a tree. I sat at the base and looked up at him.

He stood in the clearing, a black silhouette, his head tilted back and did not make a move for a long time. Finally, without looking at me, he reached within his long coat and behind, at belt level, and his hand reappeared with a gun. I didn't know anything about guns. All I knew was it looked menacing.

I gasped, clutching both hands hard to my chest now.

Then the strangest thing happened. Still looking upward, Bast raised his gun-hand up and up. Toward the tree. The sky. I heard a click. Then two cracks. *Bang. Bang.*

My body jerked twice.

Bast lowered his hand and put his gun back in his hidden holster. Next, still not sparing one glance my way, he began to dig.

For a long time I watched as he made a hole big enough for a human being. Sweat began to shine on his face. His coat was smudged with dirt and dust.

When he was done, he set the shovel aside and opened the package with the large sheet of plastic. He placed it in the grave, then began to cover it with dirt.

What the fuck?

He was making it look like he'd done the work. Did everything but shoot me.

When he was done, he leaned against the shovel and finally his eyes met mine. Cold. Unreadable.

"Stay here," he said. "I know you don't have any food or water but I'll be back. I'll try not to take more than a few hours. If I don't return, you're going to have to find your own way from here."

My breaths heaved. "What? You're—you're not going to kill me?"

"I know it will be hard, but you can walk. Hopefully, it won't come to that. I'll be back."

"B—but I don't even know where I am." I was still processing that this was happening. That what I was perceiving was true. Bast was not going to shoot me. Bast was saving my life.

"You're in the foothills of Mount Orro."

Like that helped. I blinked up at him.

"If I'm not back by nightfall, go back to the road. Can you find it?"

I shook my head. I knew nothing about navigating forests. I had been raised on the streets. As Bast stared at me with those unfathomable eyes, I nodded. "I can do it," I said. I knew the direction we'd come, but now everything looked the same. I'd find a way.

"Good. But for now, shut up and stay put."

His footfalls receded into the undergrowth and then I was alone.

Still in shock, I stared up into the dawn. Through the thick trees I could see patches of lightening sky, pale green tinged with pink.

I thought I'd never see another sunrise. I was wrong.

Chapter Six

Bast

"Did he squeal much?" Stone offered me a cigarette.

I waved my hand, declining. "No."

"Damn. He was a cute one. I'd have had my way with him first, I think."

The car turned onto the highway, heading back to the city. "I'm sure you would have."

Stone turned all the way facing me. "You know, Bast, you're a real cold shit. I'm thinking you don't like me."

I met his gaze. "You're not on any special list. I don't like anyone."

He frowned, mulling over my words in his slow brain. "Oh."

Stone was nothing to me, and the last item on my list of thoughts, if he even made the list at all. Topmost item: What had I just done?

Saved an innocent man, that's what. More, I'd saved a guy who, when he looked at me even though he knew nothing about me except I was one of his captors, communicated to me a sort of unconditional trust I wasn't sure how to interpret. As if, somehow, he knew I wanted to be on his side, wanted to help.

All I'd done was give him a damned soda. And well, then, saved his life.

But something else was there, too. Something invisible and compelling that woke more than a cop's protective instinct. Flashes of him sitting, weak and in pain, at the trunk of the pine at the burial site kept invading my mind. His hair in slick hanks hanging in his face. His muscular chest exposed from the black vest he wore that was a size too small. His injured hand clutched tight in his good hand, his feet bare and covered in dirt and leaves, the left one bloody.

There was so much I had to do now. So much I couldn't forget. I was responsible for him, as well as keeping him a secret from both Myre and Sam.

I'd killed for Myre before. For the job with the force and my job with Myre. Both occupations mixing into one and the same after two years undercover. But today I'd decided not to. No more.

Sam was going to be furious with me if he found out. But I'd asked him for help and he'd let me down. Left me in a position to do the dirty work on a guy taking the blame for *my* deeds.

Several times this past year I'd told Sam I was done. He needed to pull me back into the fold. Send me elsewhere. Another city. Another life. He'd convinced to hold out a few more months.

Sam I could handle. But if Myre ever found out Kee was still alive, I'd be dead before I drew my next breath.

I had plans to make. I could not afford one wrong move.

The drive back to the casino seemed endless. On Myre's orders, the driver had to stay within the speed limit at all times. Our people could not be pulled over for even the most minor of infractions.

Myre was already suspicious of everyone, including those closest to him. He did not trust any interaction with cops. Yet strangely, he trusted me. I worked hard to build that. I was the force's most valuable asset concerning this case at the moment.

Now, this one act, saving this Omega, put everything in jeopardy for me. But I found I did not care.

As the sunrise turned the sky lavender and pink, I kept thinking about Kee alone in that forest. Kee in his shock and hurt. Kee looking up at me as if I were the worst monster and best ally combined. And I supposed it was the truth.

50

As we pulled into the garage and rolled down to the private level, I was already undoing my seatbelt.

"In a hurry?" asked Stone.

"Yes. Apparently. My sleep was interrupted. Last night." I'd learned early on short, clipped sentences chased him away.

"Boss is gonna want a report."

"Of course."

We rode the elevator to the second floor which was all offices. I strode quickly toward Myre's, Stone two paces back trying to keep up. It might be too early yet for Myre to be there, but it was protocol to check in.

Through the glass windows of the first office, I saw him, the old man, dressed to the nines and looking fresh and clear-eyed despite his age at just after five-fucking-thirty in the morning.

Myre rose as we approached, opening the door when we arrived. He gestured for Stone to wait outside and ushered me in.

"Sebastian." His smile broke more wrinkles into his skin. His hand grazed my back, friendly and supportive, steering me to the chair by his desk.

I sat as he walked to his side of the desk and gracefully seated himself.

"So. How did things go?" He projected a casual manner, as if someone's life had not just been lost. "I see you did some digging." He waved a hand at my dusty clothes.

"Everything is fine, sir. You have no more worries."

"Exactly what I like to hear. I know you don't like Stone, but he pulled his weight?"

"Yes, sir."

"I hope he helped you. I know he can be lazy about such things."

"He helped just fine, sir."

"Good. It's done so nothing will crop back up in the springtime? Everything in its place?" Myre's despicable nature no longer surprised me, or even raised my blood pressure one mark.

"Yes."

"The Omega told me many interesting things when you were on your break. I'd like your perspective."

I tilted my head slightly, feigning interest. "Such as?"

"That he knew nothing about my cousin's activities. Swore to it, even after Merch broke his toe."

I kept my eyes trained straight on him, unflinching. "And you believed him?"

"He wasn't the kind to hold out in such a situation. Give him money or a big dick and he was the type to roll over. Pain should have made things even quicker and easier. But he stuck to his story."

"Dill and Guff played hard. Threw around a lot of cash. Kee was not the only Omega they rented," I offered.

"Yes. So I'm going to make it your job to find out more on this situation. Who else in their circles might be talking to the cops? Who else is a big talker?"

"You know all the names of the CI Omegas on the streets. You make sure your guys stay away. I wouldn't know where to start."

"Well, use that creative brain of yours. I didn't hire you for your muscle alone, not like Stone or Merch. I expect more from you."

I thought quickly. "I could track Kee's friends. Do you still have his phone?"

Myre smiled slowly, reaching beneath his desk. The sound of a drawer sliding outward followed. "I should never underestimate you." He placed the phone on the edge of his desk. "I need to get rid of it anyway. If anyone misses him, they could track it."

"I'll copy the information I need and get rid of it," I said, getting up and moving forward to take the phone.

"Don't just get rid of it. Destroy it," Myre ordered.

"I will, sir."

I turned to go. Myre's voice stopped me. "Sebastian." He never used my nickname.

I swiveled back to face him.

"You did good today." He nodded at me, his version of pinning an award on a lapel. As if we were children. As if we were all fuck-ups until we finally got something right.

"I won't forget it," he added. "If you need anything, do not hesitate to ask. Your clothes, for example. Burn them. You can get more at Poe's on my tab."

Poe's was one of the finest men's clothing shops in the entire city.

"Thank you, sir."

"You take the rest of the day off," he added.

I nodded.

"Send Stone in on your way out."

It was too easy to think of all this as just business. Too many times I'd forget where I was, who I was, because a lot of Myre's business was straight-forward. The casino ran strictly to the parameters of the country's laws. No figure or tax item was ever out of place. As for the illegal drugs and firearms Myre smuggled, well, mostly it all ran smooth as the casino, with trusted men and paid off guys on the inside, both in customs, the police force, the courts and the city council.

But I had supposedly just killed a guy. The casualness of it all ended there. I was very clear in this moment of exactly who I was and what I was doing.

I went to my guest suite, had the quickest shower ever and bagged my clothes. I changed into clean new clothes nearly identical to the ones I was tossing away. My closet was full of long black coats, and suits Myre had bought me over the years. Either he forgot he paid for so much for me, or he wanted me to have a large wardrobe. The gold watch on my wrist was a testament to his trust in me. But I'd earned every fucking bit of it.

I had arrived at a superstore one-stop-shop by eight a.m. It took me less than two hours to shop for everything I required.

I'd made a careful list. I considered various facets of Kee's needs. I had fantastic peripheral vision, and on the entire ride to the foothills and our walk into the undergrowth, I'd made a mental note of his every injury. I was a good judge of size and I estimated his clothing necessities as well. I couldn't pick and choose to dress him as I might have liked, if I cared. I didn't have the time. But I threw in my cart a few packages of underwear and socks. Shoes were a problem. They'd have to wait. He might have a broken toe anyway, so I opted for soft slippers in a large.

The food was another matter. I had stuff at my apartment, so he wouldn't starve, but when I fetched him, he'd need water. I put a six pack in the cart, along with a couple packs of energy bars. On a whim, I added fruit, chips and chocolate. All quick energy foods. Kee might not be in the mood to eat when I arrived, but once I got him settled at my place, I could make sure he was well-fed and had snacks for when I was gone.

It had been a long time since I'd had an Omega to care for. The instinct rose up in me nearly against my own will, as if I were some animal responding to hormones alone. We all were animals, of course, Alpha and Omega alike, but control had to hold some weight, and I liked to think I wielded it better than most.

The drive took half an hour. The hike into the woods was fast. I practically sprinted through the dense foliage, following my own tracks from earlier in the day. It was hotter now that it was closer to midday. My heart pounded as I crashed through bushes and branches and scattered leaves.

Insects and birds went silent yet again as I made my way to the burial site. I had a fear that someone might've checked up on me and found Kee sitting against the tree trunk still alive. My daydream nightmare was that Kee had been caught and killed, and Myre's man now lay in wait for me to shoot me and dump me into the same shallow grave.

The straps of my supply pack dug into my shoulders. I was in good shape, but I hated hiking. Camping. Anything like that. That sought after activity was not for me.

I had noted landmarks at dawn. They looked different now, the shadows falling in different directions.

Finally, I found the small clearing and saw the loose dirt where I'd put the fake grave—a grave I'd dug in case anyone from Myre's gang did come back this way and wanted to see for themselves a body had been buried.

I jogged forward, glancing toward the base of the big pine. I blinked twice. My mouth dropped open.

Kee was not there.

Chapter Seven

Kee

I woke from my doze to the sound of branches breaking. Something big was out there, and the noise it made grew louder.

Whatever it was appeared to be coming my way.

I scrambled awkwardly to a standing position, hopping once as my sore toe throbbed from any weight put on that bare foot. My broken finger was numb, luckily. Dazed, thirsty, I still had the wherewithal to back as silently as possible behind the tree and move away from the clearing. I ducked behind a large bush with little white flowers. I had no idea what the plant was, or even if it might be poisonous, but I had bigger problems right now.

If the thing in the forest was Bast coming back for me, that would be wonderful. Or, if not wonderful, better than nothing. But I couldn't count on that. My trust in anything good happening for me right now was running low at this point.

He did say he'd be back. But he was also a gangster. Someone who committed crimes and looked out for himself first. And obeyed his boss's orders.

I crouched down, wincing at my toe again, my body shivering from the adrenalin of what I might see come crashing into the clearing. My face itched. My body felt grubby and hot, yet cold and damp at the same time. My jeans were totally soiled, but dry at least, and I was beyond being embarrassed about that right now.

I waited. The sounds went soft, then loud again, as if whoever it was hesitated. I held my breath and closed my eyes, counting to ten. It was a stupid habit but it had helped me through bad times when I was a kid, and now counting seemed like a good idea.

I heard it come into the pile of leaves at the break of the clearing where Bast and I had stumbled along. Slowly, I opened my eyes.

The Alpha stood there glancing around, a sour look of disbelief creasing his forehead and narrowing his eyes. His knee-length coat had been cleaned—or it was a brand new one—and he had changed his clothing underneath as well. The shirt and trousers looked new and shiny black.

"Fuck!" The word reverberated through the air like a shotgun blast.

"Bast," I croaked. I started to stand up.

He cocked his head in my direction. "Kee?"

"I'm over here."

He ran toward me just as I came out from behind the bush, and steadied me with a hand on my upper arm. It squeezed tighter than was comfortable, but I took comfort from the touch anyway.

"What are you doing?" He practically growled.

"I heard something coming. I wasn't sure it was you, so I hid."

"Of course. Yes. That was smart."

"Yeah."

"Are you well? Can you walk with me out of here?"

He wasn't one for niceties, I noted. Straight to the point.

"I don't know." My feet were bare and hurting. And I was dying of thirst. I couldn't recall how long it had taken us to hike in here from the road. Ten minutes I might be able to do. An hour? No.

Bast let go of me and stepped back, swinging a small pack from his shoulder. He deftly opened it and handed me a bottle of water. "Here. Drink this."

I grabbed it with my good hand but fumbled to unscrew the cap.

"Give it to me." Bast grabbed it and opened it for me.

I downed almost three-quarters of the contents in a few long gulps.

"Slow down a little," Bast said.

I was half-hung over and tired and in pain. And probably still in shock. I couldn't slow down if I tried.

Bast brought out something that looked like a candy bar. My stomach was unreasonable about that, tightening at the sight of it, upset as if I'd eaten a meal that didn't agree. I shook my head.

"For instant energy. It's here if you need it." Bast threw it back into the bag, then reached in and pulled out a pair of blue, soft booties.

For a moment I thought I was dreaming. Not a nightmare—or daymare—this time. But a real dream of something soft and comforting. This man had obviously brought these slippers with me in mind. And they were brand new because the tags were still on them.

"These should cushion your feet for the walk. I wasn't sure you'd be ready for shoes and anyway I didn't know your size. These are a large."

"They will be fine." I tossed my empty water bottle aside, which Bast immediately picked up with a frown, and took them, reaching down and putting one on my sore foot to see how it felt.

It was wonderful. Like a pillow surrounding my whole foot as well as the ankle. These were boot slippers that reached halfway up my calf. I stepped gingerly, balanced, and put on the second slipper to match. I hated to think about getting blood all over them, but I had no choice.

I looked up. Bast was staring at me with a dark, unreadable look, intense enough to make me uncomfortable under normal circumstances. But right now I gloried in the attention, and that he had kept his word and returned for me.

I glanced up. "When we get back to the car, what are you going to do with me?"

"Do with you?"

I nodded.

"You will have to come with me. You can't be seen. If anyone from Myre's group sees you, they'll know I didn't do my job. If the cops see you, same difference."

"What do you mean if the cops see me? Shouldn't I go to them for help?"

Bast shook his head. "Myre has his spies everywhere. They can't protect you."

"But I'm no danger."

"You are correct. You aren't a danger to anyone and never were. But you are *in* danger. So I have to be sure you aren't seen."

"That sounds like a plan." I had no other options. I would go with this Alpha over a cliff right now if he told me to do it. Everything about him shouted *no* and *danger.* His lack of humor, his dark gazes, his black clothes.

He had the look of an Alpha you didn't dare fuck with. Gruff. No-nonsense. Yet there was an appeal to his stark, angular features and soft black hair greased straight back from his face. His hairline was a neat, curving line into his sideburns, his eyebrows sleek as if painted on, his lips a perfect pink bow.

Unlike Myre, he had no wrinkles, his skin unblemished and taut against his cheekbones. I couldn't tell his age, but he didn't look old even though he had a rather jaded air about him. All in all, if one looked through the icy exterior, he was quite handsome.

I was going to stick as close to him as glue. I could have done far, far worse for myself.

"We don't have time for first aid but here." From the pack, Bast produced what looked sort of like a Popsicle stick and some tape. He had the thing in place on my flattened and bloody finger before I could take a breath.

It hurt like all the hells in all the worlds. When he touched it, pain shot through my arm and into my head making me taste a metallic coating in the back of my throat.

I gave a little moan.

"Let's go. We should not spend more time here than necessary."

Yes! Take me away from here now! Aloud, I said, "I never want to come back here for as long as I live."

"We won't."

The assurance was all I needed. I was going with him even if I had to stumble through thorns and snakes to get there. Even if he was broody and never smiled. This Alpha had saved my life and I would be forever grateful to him.

Bast kept his hand on my elbow as if to steer me, but he was also helping me keep my balance over rocks and clumps of weeds. If he hadn't returned, and I was left on my own, I don't know how I would have gotten out of this forest. I was completely turned around.

The slippers cushioned my feet, helping with the pain, but flopped a little, also tripping me up. But it was awesome that Bast had the thought to bring them to me.

My head swam as we walked. The woods were not pretty and leafy and piney, but masses of green barriers, blurred, all looking the same. The air should have smelled fresh, pollinated by old and new leaves and late summer flowers, but instead all I smelled was my own sour fear

I tried to focus on Bast, his scent trailing out, leading me. Despite the hard and dark exterior, everything about him now meant my safety, and so his scent reminded me of clean sheets, a warm fire, and hot cocoa on a winter night. It was completely incongruous with the current heat of the day.

When I stumbled too hard, he caught me.

"I think I need to stop for a second," I said. I reached up to my face to wipe at my eyes and my hand came away wet. Was I crying? No. Everything would be fine now so I had no reason. Still, my eyes stung.

He stood beside me as I took deep breaths, leaning against him. After a moment, he said, "Ready?"

"Yes."

"It's only a few more minutes."

To him that was nothing. To me, in my condition, it was an eternity.

When we finally reached his car, I wasn't surprised to see it was also black, like everything surrounding him. He helped me into the passenger seat, tucking my feet in, making sure nothing was hanging out, then handed me another water and a chocolate bar.

"Eat that if you can," he instructed. "It will give you quick energy which you need for the time being."

I held both items in my lap, still favoring my hand with the broken finger.

When Bast got into the driver's seat, he glanced at me, frowning, then took the water from me and opened it. He did the same with the candy, handing both back to me.

I drank some more, then took a bite of the chocolate. The sugar rush went through me fast as I swallowed. It was the best thing I'd ever tasted and I gobbled another bite.

Bast drove down the road, checking over his shoulder every few minutes.

"Were we followed?" The question left my heart cold as I waited for an answer.

"No. I made sure of it."

Relief swept through me, almost as good as the sugar rush. "Where are we going?"

"My place."

"Is it safe there?"

"If you don't do anything stupid like be seen."

I bowed my head. "You're hiding me."

"You can't go out in public."

"Ever?"

"Not for a very long time. Not until I figure some things out."

"So I'll be staying with you? Or are you dropping me somewhere else later on?"

He frowned but did not look at me as he replied, tone flat, "With me."

"Oh. Okay."

"There is nowhere else for you to go."

I should have thanked him. Certainly, I was grateful. But my throat closed up in another surge of panic. My life as I knew it was over. All my street friends would wonder where I was. I wouldn't be able to contact them. I wouldn't be able to do anything.

When I could speak again, I asked, "What happened to my phone?"

"I destroyed it. No one will be able to track you. You cannot contact anyone from your old life. Do you understand?"

I nodded once, balancing the chocolate bar, which was melting where my fingers clutched it. My good hand shook.

"I am very serious here. It cannot be known that you are still alive."

But how long would that last? I wanted to ask so many questions, but I guess now we had a lot of time for all that. Right now I wanted to bury my head in the sand. I wanted to go away in my head, escape, pull a blanket all the way over myself.

"You don't happen to have any steam." My voice came out far too hesitant for what I was asking.

"No drugs. That's one of my rules."

I hadn't agreed to any rules, but he was doing all this for me. I needed to respect that. But rarely had I done what needed to be done in my life.

"It's going to be hard for me." Now I spoke in just above a whisper. "I pretty much had steam and alcohol every day."

"I am quite aware you are an addict."

An addict. It sounded so crass. So simple. It was much more complicated than that. At least to me.

Everything hurt. I took another bite of chocolate, but it got all over me. I looked frantically around for somewhere to set it. Bast must have seen, because he pointed at a bag between us situated in a hole in the center console. It was obviously for trash.

I dropped the candy in there, sad to see it go, and rubbed my sticky fingers on my already soiled jeans. There was no chance of saving them so it didn't matter if I used them as a napkin.

The car jolted as Bast came onto the main highway. Suddenly, there were other cars everywhere and I became intensely paranoid. Would someone see me?

"The windows are blackened," said Bast, as if reading my mind.

I took a deep breath and fiddled with my water. My finger, splinted, had stopped sending me shocking stabs of pain now that it was immobilized. Maybe there was hope for me yet.

But I still worried about everything. Namely, right now, the drug withdrawal. I had never tried to go clean before. I used daily, some days more intensely than others, and I craved it. Alcohol wasn't my problem. It was steam. When I needed it badly enough, I could taste it. My mind latched onto that and demanded. My body hungered. I would do anything to get another fix when I reached that point.

But now I would have none of that.

My rational mind reminded me. *But you have your life!*

Maybe it would have been better off for everyone, Bast included, if I'd died. The burden for him of hiding me—I couldn't imagine it. It was a huge risk he was taking. Life and death. I didn't like being responsible for anyone but myself. I'd lived that way on the streets since I was sixteen. No ties, no rules, no responsibilities. It was why I couldn't keep anything for any amount of time, like a car or an apartment. I got things when I needed them any way I could, and tossed the rest over my shoulder.

I didn't really want to get clean. But now I had no choice. Later, maybe Bast would discuss with me the method. Like doing it slow. That meant I could have steam, but in less and less increments. Yeah, that sounded like a plan. But I wasn't going to bring it up at this moment.

I rubbed at the plastic label on the water bottle, trying to ground myself.

"Where do you live?" I asked. I needed to break the discomfort in my brain.

"As far away from the casino as possible while still within a reasonable driving distance."

"Why?"

"Because I like my privacy."

I leaned back on the headrest and my eyes drifted shut. Only for a moment. But when I opened them we were pulling into a private lot lined by trees.

Bast got out and came around to my side, opening the door for me. I was so groggy I couldn't find the door handle.

I looked up at him through bright noon sunlight. "Won't people see me?"

"Most people who live here work during the day. But hurry if you can."

Bast steered me up a cement walkway lined with perfectly square, trimmed hedges. His apartment was on the first floor, and a single short step led up to the door. He quickly unlocked it and pushed the door open, shoving me inside in front of him.

I blinked to clear my vision. It was dark inside, full of shadows, and I nearly tripped as I crossed the threshold. The air felt cool against my hot skin. My cheeks began to itch, and the pain throughout my body returned in various aches and sharp stabs. It all flooded in probably because in this moment I realized I was somewhere safe, somewhere I could let all the tension fall away and crumble.

The door closed behind me with a bang and I jumped.

Bast laid a warm hand on my shoulder. It felt comforting but in reality it was his way of steering me where he wanted me to be.

I was ready to crash. I hadn't really slept in over twenty-four hours. Dozing by the tree amid the leaves, dirt and tickly ferns didn't count.

"The bathroom is through there." Bast pointed to a short hall. "And the bedroom."

"You only have one bedroom?"

"Yes. And you can have the bed. I'll sleep on the couch. When I'm here."

"When you're here? You mean you're gone a lot?"

"Yes. That is what I said."

He sounded grouchy. Maybe he was as tired as I was. Maybe he got no sleep either. But what freaked me out a little was the idea that I'd be alone. A lot. I didn't do alone well. Not without some help from steam. Or alcohol. Or sex.

But right now, my biggest worry was getting to a bed. And dealing with my pain.

"I have supplies here. After you shower I can disinfect and wrap your finger better, and your toe."

I didn't know if I had energy for a shower, but I didn't argue. I went into the bathroom and started to strip. I didn't have much on: my vest, my dirtied jeans. I went commando so nothing underneath.

I left my clothes in a pile on the floor, not for a moment inhibited or bothered by the fact that Bast was in the tiny room with me, turning on the water and testing it with his hand. He held the door while I stepped into the stall and under the running water.

Warmth seeped into my skin and the pounding of the water on my back released all my tension. I wanted to cry. And laugh. This must be what paradise feels like, I decided. Water pounding all around warm and serene and secure.

I found some soap and shampoo and used liberal amounts. My splint got wet but it didn't seem to hurt it. The tape would moisten and come off later, but Bast said he had more supplies. The cuts on my skin, however, stung like hell.

Damp hair in my eyes, I could still see a dark shadow standing in front of the fogged-glass shower door. Waiting.

It was a rather strange sensation for me, knowing I was naked and bathing and there was an Alpha waiting for me but not to have sex. Not to do whatever he wanted and then toss me away. But to take care of me. Even if Bast behaved in a detached and clipped manner, he had done everything to save me. He'd even brought a pack to the burial site full of supplies. Water. Food. First aid. Like he cared. Like he felt responsible for me, or something.

When I realized I could barely stand, I turned off the water, wincing as my bad hand tweaked with pain, and pushed open the door. I stumbled out and almost into Bast's arms. He had a towel out and unfolded, and shoved it at me.

Funny; it was the kindest thing anyone had done for me in, well, forever. Well, there had been Tarin. He'd been kind. He'd tried to help me in many ways, but I wouldn't let him.

Now, I had no choice. I was a mess and I needed all the help I could get.

I grabbed the towel and began to blot it over my body as Bast turned away and fiddled in some drawers at the counter. One by one, he laid things out in a neat line by the sink. A new toothbrush. Toothpaste. Soap. A razor (though I had never needed one). Fresh hand towels and washcloth. A plastic bottle of aspirin. I figured it would be that and that alone for pain. Bast had made it clear there would be no harder drugs for me.

The withdrawal was not going to be fun, but for now I was okay in that regard.

"Dry off and put this on." Bast handed me a lightweight, rather sheer pair of white drawstring sleep pants. "When you're done, come into the bedroom and I'll take a better look at your injuries."

Yes, sir! I had an instinct to say it, but I kept my mouth shut. I was too exhausted for humor or games anyway.

It was hard to tie the drawstring. My fingers wouldn't cooperate. I ended up pulling it tight with a single knot that loosened as soon as I took a step forward. The sleep pants rode low on my hips. I didn't care. I was grateful for the shower and the clean clothes. Grateful to be with a man who seemed intent on keeping me healthy and alive. Why he was like this when the others were hell-bent on not only causing me pain but also causing my death, was going to be an interesting tale to sort out. Later.

I held my pants at the hip with my good hand to keep them on, and entered the bedroom.

Bast sat on the edge of a neatly made bed. Sheets and pillowcases were piled by the door. He must have re-made the bed while I was in the shower.

Normally, I loved it when Alphas gave me things, or catered to me. An Alpha might allow me to have his bed for the night and I'd take it. I wanted whatever I could get. I deserved to be treated well. My sense of entitlement was brazen. Alphas got what they wanted from me, so I should have what I desired in return. Soft clean sheets included.

But Bast was different. I was already indebted to him and it would only grow deeper. Guilt swept through me. It was an alien feeling. I lived my life with no regrets, no looking back.

Now I stood in a room I did not want to be in with no hope for immediate escape. My life remained in danger. How long I would be here was unknown.

"I—I can take a spot on the floor, make a bed out of blankets and pillows."

Bast stared at my waist where my hand gathered my waistband. Slowly, he raised his eyes up over my belly and chest and finally to my face.

"You're badly bruised."

I looked down. I had red marks turning purple at the edges on my stomach and left side. My ribs ached but they were the least of it. The toe throbbed. The Alpha who'd broken my finger had also used his fist on me a few times. One time he hit so hard it made me retch.

"Come here," Bast said.

When I didn't move, he rolled his eyes and waved me over, his hand jerking back fast.

I went to him and stood in front of him. He did not hesitate to shove my hand aside and take up the drawstring, tying a quick bow. His hand strayed very close to my crotch as he did so, but he gave no indication he noticed.

"Sit up in the bed, all the way at the head," he instructed.

I climbed in as he turned to face me, still seated on the edge. Without asking permission, he took my injured foot in hand. He had a box beside him containing bandages, tape, scissors, and various different colored bottles.

With a square of gauze dipped in something that looked like lube, Bast wiped at my very purple, still oozing and throbbing toe. The medicine he used on it smelled of cherries. He was cursory and professional, but his touch came gentle. He didn't twist my toe or bump it, but bathed it with light, slow dabs.

"This is just a topical." He sounded almost bored. "It will numb it to some extent. I don't think it's broken, just cut, but I'll also give you aspirin for the pain and that's all you get."

I didn't argue. Whatever he gave seemed like a gift after the past sixteen hours.

Bast then proceeded to wrap the toe and then the front half of my foot in thicker, cottony gauze. "This will cushion it as you move around."

I swallowed, my throat thick.

When he finished, he grabbed for my injured hand. I let him. He took off the sopping wet tape and re-splinted the finger with new tape, first wrapping it so it, like the toe, was cushioned.

"You've done this before?" I asked.

"Never." He did not look up.

"Well, you're doing a great job."

When he was done, he leaned back. "You will let me know if the pain on your ribs and abdomen gives you more trouble."

I nodded.

"I don't want anyone else involved, but if I have to call a doctor, I know someone who will be discreet."

Next, Bast handed me a bottle of cold water and two aspirin from a bottle in his first aid box. I downed them in one gulp.

"Are you hungry?" he asked.

I still felt sick to my stomach. The bites of chocolate I'd eaten in the car roiled around inside me. "No. I just feel like I can't even sit up anymore."

"Lie down, then." He pulled the covers away, revealing the sheets of the just-made bed. More guilt. More discomfort at my dire situation. I usually only felt deserving of care like this when Alphas paid me and got something in return.

Bast's voice came again in its usual drone. As if he didn't care, though his actions showed otherwise. "I don't have to be back at work until tomorrow. If you need anything, I'll be here."

I scooted under the covers, aware even more, as the softness enveloped me, of my vulnerable state. My nakedness, save a thin pair of sleep pants, was about more than my body right now. My arms and legs shook. I closed my eyes as yet more tears heated the edges, slicking my eyelashes.

When I lay back on the pillows, a loud sigh escaped my lips. Hands drew covers over me and the sheets were crisp and cool against my chest. Finally, I could rest and know no harm would come to me. Finally, I could sleep.

The bed shifted as Bast got up and I heard his footfalls on the rug as he crossed the room. I blearily opened my eyes to see he hadn't left, but had gone to an armchair in one corner.

His gaze remained on me. He seemed to be glaring, but I didn't mind. I took comfort just knowing he'd probably be there when I woke.

Chapter Eight

Bast

When I woke, the room was dim. I'd dozed off in the recliner. The afternoon had gone.

My stomach growled.

I glanced at the lump in my bed. Kee slept on, curled on his right side, covers thrown back from his shoulder and arm showing a lot of golden and trimly muscled skin.

At some point, as I sat vigil over him, he'd tossed a bit and moaned in his sleep. But nothing too terrible. I'd adjusted his covers once; he didn't wake.

He would sleep for some hours more, I was sure. I got up and used the bathroom, then went into the kitchen and made myself a fresh pot of coffee, and some scrambled eggs and toast. My inner clock was completely off. I had breakfast for dinner far too often. And dinner at six a.m.

I brought my food into the bedroom on a tray. I didn't want to stray too far from Kee. It was a weird feeling, not one I usually had. Protective? Perhaps, but only insofar as my job had compromised him and I was responsible.

I'd killed before. To cement my cover. To earn Myre's trust. But those incidents had been mostly self-defense. At least that's what Sam told me to keep me grounded in the field, to keep me in a gang I felt far too much a part of lately.

When I finished my meal, I checked my texts.

Kee turned in the bed, the covers going all over the place, and moaned, then settled curled up on his other side. He now faced more toward me. The pants I'd given him were tugged down a little revealing an edge of golden hip.

Saliva built up in my mouth and I swallowed hard. My gaze did not leave his form. His hair, like a tidal wave of dark brown swept over his face. One arm stuck straight out in front of him, the injured hand thick in white wrappings. His bicep bulged beneath smooth, hairless skin.

I forced shallow breaths. If I inhaled deeply, I could smell him and that just wouldn't do. As it was, he was leaving his street-soaked peach scent all over everything in my bedroom. He also smelled hot and edgy, like distant lightning just before the rain comes and washes the world.

His scent affected me, as it would any Alpha. Nothing special here, just one more Omega essence teasing the Alpha chemical make up as biology dictated.

No, I told myself. I didn't want to take him. I didn't want to put little babies into his body. My body surged because that was the way it was made. My mind was my own and it was the meat-suit trapping that came with its own set agendas.

That wasn't me.

Besides, I had little use for Omegas on a strictly for-need basis. My Burns were clean, which meant every two months I had a bit of a fever for a day or so, and only a minimal urge to mate. It didn't make me less powerful an Alpha, simply my semen potency was half of normal range, so my chances of producing children were considerably reduced. It was a relief, actually, that I didn't have to be saddled with that responsibility. I could focus on my job.

Myre bought and sold Omegas like candy. Like the drugs he dispersed throughout the country. When I needed one, a pretty young thing was always available at no charge to me, no questions asked. I didn't like the set up but I used it as did all his crew. I knew he also sold them to secret and particular underground kink establishments, and many were never heard from again. He could have done that with Kee, but he'd chosen to silence him. Forever.

Myre had no children and I never asked why. Or maybe he did have them, but never raised them or claimed them as his heirs.

As I watched Kee sleep, lips slightly parted to form a pink oval, I noted his beauty. I'd be a liar if I didn't admit to myself I noticed. But Omega pretty boys were a dime a dozen. It meant nothing to me, his looks, his deep green cat's eyes that were exotic as hell, and his filled-out body that many Alpha's would envy.

It wasn't right that he should die at Myre's order. But now, here he was. Exactly the sort of extra complication I didn't need in my life right now. Of course I was happy not to kill him, but what had I gotten myself into?

As night came on, Kee continued to sleep, his rest deep now, very still. I dozed away another hour, then another.

When I opened my eyes, Kee was sitting up in my bed staring at me through the curving shadows cast by the hall light.

I leaned forward. "You're awake."

"At first I didn't know where I was." He spoke in an almost-whisper. "Then I saw you sitting there."

"I suppose you will be hungry."

Kee cocked his head, a dark silhouette that even in this dimness spelled trouble for me. I could feel it in my bones.

"Do you have my phone?" he asked.

"You asked that before. I told you it had to be destroyed. For one thing, it has a GPS."

He said nothing.

"You had over twenty texts from someone named Tarin. Do I have to worry? Will he be looking for you?"

"No. Well, maybe. But not officially. Not involving the authorities or anything."

"Who is he?"

Kee shrugged.

"I'm not prying. I couldn't care at all about your personal life. But I need to know these things."

"Just a friend. That's all."

"That's all? Having that attitude almost got you killed."

Kee threw back his head. "Are you one of those people who blames the victim?"

72

"If the victim is at fault, then, yes."

"Think you're such a badass Alpha." The words came mumbled, but I heard them loud and clear.

"Curb your behavior or you'll find out."

He let out a loud laugh that threatened to curdle the air. "I have been finding out about bad Alphas since I was fourteen."

"You think you can handle yourself."

A shrug. "Didn't care much. But yeah. Figured I was headed for a short life anyway."

"The information I have on you says you're twenty-five, so yes, I'd say that's a short life-span."

"I may be twenty-five, but I don't look a day over twenty-three." He laughed at his own quip.

Kee had the kind of laugh that held an inner echo, like emptiness existed behind it on the verge of encompassing him. I almost asked him how he came to be on the streets, where he originated from. But I stopped myself. I didn't need to know anything about him. I just needed to keep him hidden and out of trouble until I squared some things with Sam. Maybe six more months and Myre would be out of the way.

Right now, six months seemed like a lifetime.

Chapter Nine

Kee

"Ta-da!" I lay back on the living room couch and tossed the fist-sized rubber ball into the air and caught it over and over in my good hand.

It was late evening now.

Cooking smells and sizzling sounds came from the kitchen. Hamburger. The scent of pre-packaged rolls in the oven. At the moment, it looked like Bast wanted to cook for me. Fine with me.

I'd found the ball on a table by the couch, and when I lay back I saw the side wall was dotted with little black marks where the ball had been thrown against it a hundred or maybe a thousand times. I tried to imagine Bast lying here on the couch and tossing the ball, bored or pissed. It was so funny to think an Alpha like that, so controlled, practically emotionless, would be reduced to such a silly, childish habit.

My stomach growled. I could definitely eat now that I'd slept. What I really wanted was a hit of steam. Just a small one.

But my life as I knew it was over. Damn, this was not going to be fun. I tossed the ball harder, higher and missed it. It landed on the glass coffee table with a loud crack, knocking over a dusty red glass candle holder that had no candle in it.

I sat up. The coffee table and holder were intact.

Bast came into the kitchen doorway, frowning.

"Don't worry." I slid off the couch until my butt hit the floor and grabbed up the ball, holding it up. "Nothing's broken."

"Dinner is ready."

I stood up, wincing at my sore toe, and wandered into the kitchen. I still had no shirt and only the thin pants, but if Bast didn't care, then neither would I.

There was a dingy table by a window that looked out on a dirty white wall. There were two chairs. Bast had set two plates and some cutlery there, so I sat.

He brought the skillet over to the table and dumped a burger patty onto my plate, and pointed out the mustard and ketchup. Then he put a plate of rolls and some butter in the center.

I looked around me. The kitchen was white with forest green countertops, clean but old-looking. The floor was worn, white tile. The window had cobwebs around the edges.

I helped myself to a roll, split it open and doused it with butter. It smelled heavenly. When I took a bite, it was as if my body absorbed it and I barely had to chew it.

When Bast sat down with his own plate of food, I studied him a little further. Diamonds on both pinkies. Dark garments that looked tailored, maybe even designer labeled. Hair perfect and greased back save a few curls at the ends. He looked like a lot of Alphas: fit, healthy and superior in his haughty expression.

But this place, this apartment, it didn't fit.

"I thought you'd be richer." I spoke with my mouth full, chewing rapidly.

A smoldering glance. Eyes darker than that wrinkled old guy who was his boss.

"I guess you spend a lot of time at the hotel and casino, then?"

"I have my own suite there."

For some reason, that admission panicked me. I took another bite to hide my reaction. "So I'm going to be here on my own a lot, then?"

He didn't answer but focused intently on preparing his food. Butter on the hot rolls, mustard and a sprinkling of onions on his patty.

The next bite of my own roll went down hard. I didn't do *alone* very well. I liked company. Using cash, I rented Omega-friendly apartments or hotel rooms only for sleeping.

Otherwise, I was a party sort of guy. I found my way from Alpha to Alpha, house to house, very rarely alone.

"So, I guess silence means *yes*." I poked at my burger. "Burgers usually have buns. And stuff like lettuce, tomatoes and cheese."

"By all means, I'll go through McDonald's next time."

I took a bite of the meat. It was surprisingly tasty, seasoned and juicy. I wiped my mouth with a napkin and said, "What am I supposed to do all day alone? And for weeks, maybe longer?"

"I have a TV, a computer, video games."

"But no phone."

"I'll have a simple burner phone for you to call me if you have any emergency."

"Okay." I drew the word out. My stomach went hard and twisty. I knew I was being a brat. It was either this or death. Bast had done a huge thing for me. But this was not a life.

"I could move. To another city."

"Not far enough." Bast sounded bored, his deep voice almost sleepy. Did I bore him? Was I just another chore?

"Another country?"

"Do you have a passport?"

I shook my head no. "And I can't call any of my friends? Ever? Not even Tarin who just wants to know that I'm okay? In fact, maybe I could go stay there. He has a room for me. No one would have to know."

"Does he live alone?"

"No."

Bast made an annoyed sound and turned his head. "Have I not made myself clear on this matter? No one can know you're alive. Not for a while anyway."

"What about--"

"No one," he repeated.

"But they wouldn't have to know where I was."

"Do you have a death wish?"

"But I--"

"Myre has people everywhere. Spies. Informants. Computer software that can hack CCTV. He has a facial recognition program at the tips of his fingers. You've lived on the streets since you were teen. Have you never heard of him?"

I hung my head. I'd been out of my mind for a long, long time. In fact, I didn't pay attention enough to my surroundings, and rumors and gossip never interested me. Only money and fun. Sex and steam.

"But if he thinks I'm dead, he wouldn't even be looking."

Bast gestured toward the kitchen door that led to the living room. "Take your chances, then. Walk through that front door and go. See what happens."

Now he had me more scared. I frowned. "But you'll be checking on me, right? Not gone all the time. Bringing in groceries and stuff, right?"

"I'll be around." His voice softened. "Do you have any hobbies?"

"Like what?" I sounded dejected, like a child.

"I don't know. You tell me. Painting. Doing puzzles. Making macaroni pictures. I can get you glue. I can get you bags of pasta tubes."

Was Bast making a joke? I looked up to see if he had cracked even half a smile. But he was intent on his food, buttering a second roll.

My hobbies were sex and drugs. Drinking. Sleeping during the day and staying up all night. Those were my hobbies. Even now, I craved some steam. My body hadn't had time to de-tox yet, but I heard that some got the shakes when they quit, or major flu-like symptoms.

"I'll need something to get me through the steam withdrawal."

"I'll see to it."

"See to what?"

"There's medication for it. I'll get it."

"Don't you need a prescription?"

"I said I'll get it." Bast would not look at me.

If he hated me on sight, I couldn't blame him. But then, I hadn't asked him to save my life.

"Why'd you save me anyway?"

"You were innocent for one thing," he replied a little too quickly.

"How do you know that?"

"Trust me, I just do."

This was going to be a miserable unspecified time out of my life. And though Bast was attractive to me even with his acerbic tone and dark glares, he didn't seem the least bit interested in me as a person or an Omega even though I was eating dinner with him mostly naked. It was fairly clear and simple to me: he didn't like me.

I was stuck. No friends. No life. No steam. No sex. And no future, although my future prospects before all this had already been on the low end of the bar chart.

Add to that, Bast had made a fairly tasty meal, but it wasn't real cooking. I had learned to cook pretty well as a kid from even the barest available ingredients. Would he even allow me to take over the kitchen? Well, if he was going to be gone half the time, I'd be left to cook for myself, so in a way, I'd be able to take over—somewhat—the entire apartment.

Maybe after I healed, I could do some redecorating as well. It was sort of an Omega thing, nesting, but I had no plans to stay. I was merely looking at how to stave off utter boredom.

*

The front door crashed open and Bast came through laden with bags.

I jerked in surprise, my heart hammering in my chest, but had no strength to get up from the couch. My breaths came faster and faster. I hadn't seen him in a full day.

Bast put down his groceries on the coffee table and glanced over at me. "Staying out of trouble?"

"Ugh." I slung an arm over my face as I heard him walk closer to the couch.

"Did you take the pills I brought you?"

"Yeah." But the heat and clamminess would not go away. My head ached too badly to lift it.

"I recommend a cool shower."

I peeked out from under my arm, watching him turn away. This was only day four and I was in withdrawal. I feared things would only get worse before they got better.

I wasn't wrong. Bast had been gone over a day, but he'd brought dinner and I couldn't face eating a thing. I lay on the couch like a dead thing, thinking about my churning stomach, and how there was nothing left in it but the pill and the water I'd taken it with, but I still wanted to throw up, badly.

I lost all track of time. I heard Bast walking about the apartment. Once, he said to me, "Wouldn't the bed be more comfortable?"

I figured he wanted the couch so he could watch some TV. I didn't answer.

When night came, it got very dark, and I wondered if the electricity had gone out because there were no lights. It was so dark I couldn't see my hand in front of my face. I realized, finally, my eyes were tightly shut. And I was moaning.

Arms came beneath me and I was lifted into the air. Great. Maybe I would get some help. The hospital? But no, that wouldn't happen. I had the faint memory, through my fever, that I wasn't allowed to be seen.

I still couldn't open my eyes. I had the strangest sensation that I was falling apart into a thousand pieces, my arms and legs flopping, my head lolling. My legs bumped into something. I heard a low curse. Water running.

Then I was set into a tub of cool water with my drawstring pants still on. They clung everywhere to my skin, clumping, bugging me. I strained to open my eyes.

Light hit them with a fierce power, like needles stabbing my eye sockets all at once. I cried out. I felt my body thrash in

79

the water. I smelled something like vinegar, then something sweet, like fruit juice. The bandages on my hand and foot became soaked through.

Strong hands held me down. I was fighting him? I didn't mean to. My body and mind simply weren't aligned. I felt my knees bend and the bottoms of my feet slip along the tub's porcelain bottom.

But the water lapped cool against my hot skin. It encompassed me, contained me. I found myself eventually relaxing as a steady stream poured in from the faucet, making the level rise all around me, steady, brisk, invigorating.

My eyes adjusted a bit to the bright light and I saw the dark form of Bast leaning over the tub, over me, intent on keeping me submerged but aloft, holding me in place with one hand behind my neck.

I blinked away fever tears. I knew how to make it all stop. Just a little bit of steam would do it. A tiny bit. Just to take the edge off.

"I need." I couldn't finish the sentence.

"Yes, I know," came the short reply. Like he was mad. But then he always sounded like that.

"Just a tiny amount of steam and I'll be okay."

"Uh huh."

Bastard!

"I swear, just a little and that's it. Please!" I heard myself as if from far away, begging for my drugs. I knew it was pathetic, but what did I care? That was what I wanted. I was an adult. I could do what I wanted with my life. I had no prospects. Why not spend it high?

"I don't have any on hand. Sorry."

He did not sound one bit sorry!

"You can get it, though. Your boss is the supplier."

"Uh huh." He held me down as I thrashed and a wave of water came up over the lip of the tub and splashed onto his black shirt.

80

"Fuck!" I tipped my head back. Everything hurt so much. The water was nice, but not enough. "I'll blow you for it. I swear. I'm really good."

"I'm sure you would. And are. But. No." Calm. That voice. Too fucking calm.

I started to cry.

"That won't work," he said.

What an asshole! I was so fucked.

Hands cupped water over my brow and it trickled into my hair. Then, to my surprise, Bast began to wash my hair, combing his fingers through it gently, the soap slipping against my brow and my scalp. The action sent tingles throughout my body. The good feelings started to counteract the bad just enough that I could stop blubbering and start breathing deep again, start to let my body relax.

The hair washing took up long minutes where I was silent, pliant. Bast took up a cloth to wash away the shampoo that began to run down my face—and maybe brush away the tears as well. I wasn't sure of anything at that point. My mind floated in a daze.

His palm held the back of my head up as he guided me forward through the water and toward the running faucet to rinse my hair. Cool liquid threaded through my tangles. Warm hands gently squeezed hanks of my hair.

I wanted to thank this man. Hug him. Grasp onto him. He wasn't the type for that sort of thing, it seemed, but I was so grateful I wanted to climb up his body and try to fit myself inside it.

Hold me.

Just as I had that thought, arms came around me. Powerful. Strong. I wasn't a small Omega, but he lifted me from the water as if I weighed nothing.

"Think you can stand now?" He righted me, setting me on my feet but keeping his arms around me to help my balance.

My bandage on my foot flopped, half off. My knees started to give.

81

Bast held me as I grabbed around his neck to keep from falling.

"Hmm."

The little hum he made meant everything to me. A way out. Better things. Nurture. Comfort. To him, though, it probably meant only annoyance.

With a sigh, he said, "Hold onto my shoulders. Those pants need to come off."

He was going to strip me? I almost laughed, but I had no strength. I gripped the cloth of his shirt, my splint sticking out in an obscene gesture, hanging on as he undid the knot at my waist and slid the wet pants down my hips. The material clung to my skin, forcing him to bend closer to me and yank the material down. I fell toward him, my cock and balls swinging toward his chin.

Alphas were often surprised at my length and girth. A lot of them liked to ignore Omega cocks and go only for the hole. It was fine by me, but I had a cock most couldn't ignore. It made itself well-known, for which I was proud.

If Bast noticed, he made no reaction. He knelt and pulled one pant leg off, then the other, taking the foot bandage all the way off as well.

He rose back to full height. Completely nude now, I leaned against him. My wet hair trailed over my shoulders, sending cold streams of water down my back.

He stood very still for a moment, as if he couldn't decide what to do next. My forehead pressed against his rock hard chest. I felt wrung out, exhausted. Dizzy. But the nausea had receded, at least for now.

"Kee. Kee!"

I looked up, realizing he'd been calling my name. Our faces were very close and his eyes weren't really black, but a beautiful dark brown with pinpoint pupils, shining, lit up. His face had strong contours—high cheekbones, square jaw— beneath smooth, tanned skin. I noticed he was usually close-shaven, but right now he sported a dark shadow that covered his jaw and chin, outlining his lips. A pinkness slowly edged up his cheeks.

So. I did have an affect on him.

"Kee," he said again.

"I'm right here, damn it!" I could smell his breath, hot and fiery, making me want him even in my desperate condition.

"You were passing out again."

I lowered my forehead to his chest again and mumbled, "Was not."

Without anymore argument, he lifted me up. I half-shrieked, half-yelled as his arms came under my naked ass and beneath my upper back. I hugged my arms around his neck.

Without a word, he took me to the bed and lay me on it. The covers had been pulled back, the sheets crisp and clean, newly changed. I lay back on utter softness, groaning as I did so, not caring that I was entirely exposed, legs bent, cock resting on the inside of my thigh. I had little body hair, so nothing really covered me down there. My balls had to be shining pink under the lights, still wet, skin glistening.

I thought that would be it. Bast would turn out the light and leave. Instead, he took up a towel by the bedside and gently began to rub me down. Gods, it felt so good. At this point, I'd let him do whatever he wanted. The towel was fluffy and soft, the rhythm he made had me melting into the sheets as my fever abated even further and my mind gave in to simple pleasure.

He used another towel on my hair, gently lifting my head as he ran it over my tangles.

When he was done, he tossed the towels aside and stood by the side of the bed like an Alpha lording over an Omega—I couldn't think of it any other way—and stared at me.

I blinked up at him. I knew he was looking at me. I wanted him to look. I worked hard to be pretty, to be strong with a tight body and supple skin. I wasn't sure how I looked right now, though, frazzled and sick, damp from a bath, not quite put together, reeling half in and out of reality. Maybe the whole sick and helpless thing worked a little, I didn't know, but

I liked him looking. I liked that he couldn't ignore me. What I didn't like was the circumstance. Having death hanging over my head. Feeling too ill to function.

Finally, Bast drew a sheet over me to mid-chest, turned and left the room. The light remained on, and I started to call out, but soon he returned with a glass of water and some pills in the palm of his hand.

"Take this." He put a hand beneath my shoulder and helped me sit up.

"What is it?"

"Aspirin. You can't have more of the detox meds for six hours."

My hand shook as I took the pills from him, stuffed them in my mouth, and reached for the glass. I drank thirstily, draining it.

Bast took the glass from my hand, letting me lie back. "I'll get more water. It'll be on the nightstand if you need it."

"Thank you."

I closed my eyes and sleep came swiftly.

Bast must not have left the room, at least not for very long increments, because when I woke in dim light thrashing, calling out, I felt strong arms holding me down. The sheet was tangled about my legs. The pillows were strewn at my sides. My body shivered and quaked uncontrollably. Muscle cramps squeezed up and down my legs and in my abdomen.

I yelled a lot, but strong hands seemed to know where to touch. He massaged my legs until I could straighten them out. As I clutched my stomach, he gently pried my hands away and rubbed circles around my belly button, soothing me.

Exposed and naked again, I didn't care.

Eventually, I turned into his embrace. "Don't leave," I whispered.

Miraculously, his arms did not move away, and I fell back to sleep in his embrace, my face pressed to the inside of his shoulder.

Chapter Ten

Bast

"I need you here by one," Myre said.

I stared at my phone. I hated to leave Kee when he was so vulnerable, at his worst. But Myre brooked no excuses from his crew.

"Yes, sir."

It had been a hard night. I'd gotten only a few hours of sleep. Kee had been so ill at several points I'd almost called my doctor friend. I discovered he relaxed and slept easier when I was near. What I could easily do for him was keep him hydrated by making him drink lots of water, which he did not turn down, and massage away his pain and cramps.

He called out for me if I wasn't there right by his side. He probably didn't even know he was doing it, but if I could make him stop yelling by being nearby, I'd do it. No sense attracting the attention of the neighbors. If I put my arms around him, he would curl into me and sleep like a baby.

Now I had to go back into the bedroom and tell him he was on his own. It might be hours. Myre had various projects and kept me close whenever he needed me. Sometimes for days at a time. Plus, I owed a report to Sam. But that would require another surreptitious trip to the abandoned building down the block from the casino.

When would I have the time?

Maybe on the way to work I could buy a burner and use that. Once. Then get rid of it. It was more dangerous. I might be seen buying it. It might push the paranoia button on an already paranoid crime boss.

I walked into the bedroom in my bare feet. The soft shuffle of my clothing seemed too loud. I always expected the room to smell like illness and suffering, but Kee gave off his peach scent that was so nice, so wonderful I didn't want to think about it.

Most Omegas smelled from just okay to great. All Alphas experienced this attunement to Omega scent. It was in our chemistry. But this Omega's fragrance penetrated through my body leaving me overly concerned for him—more than I would be. And hungry. More than I would be.

Touching him didn't help. His skin was leaf-soft, his muscles curving in all the right places. He'd been naked before me in the bathroom, and thrown his sheets off so many times in the bed that I had memorized his body.

Yes, he was pretty. Almost too pretty. Ample in all the right places, trim everywhere else, and little to no body hair, which made him seem all the more vulnerable to me.

I was not interested in him at all. No. But I kept having to remind myself of this. It wasn't the fact that he was a street whore. I didn't care about that one way or the other. Selling yourself for sex wasn't illegal. But he was an addict. That was a problem. I didn't care for addicts.

For the time being, I might be helping him get clean, but when my job ended—and I saw that happening in less than six months—he'd go. And when he did, he'd be back to his old ways. That's how it was with addicts.

Of course I could fuck Omegas without becoming attached. But I'd never lived with one. Not for more than two days.

Kee was a street boy, sure, but along with his wild and wanton lifestyle, he had a vulnerable sweetness about him. I shouldn't have liked that about him. I shouldn't have given it a second thought.

Even though I told myself that over and over throughout the night while I'd held him to me as I slept, my cock had hardened. My skin had tingled. And that peachy fragrance nestled in the back of my throat, making my lips press tight to keep from simply leaning over him and kissing that plush, pink mouth.

I walked to the side of the bed. His hair, a shiny mess, fell into his face. I reached down and stroked it back.

His eyelids fluttered.

"Bast? Are you here?"

I took a deep breath. "Right here."

Kee held out his splinted hand. I brushed my fingertips over the top of his palm but did not take it in my own.

"Are you hungry yet?" I asked.

He struggled to sit up, the sheet falling down one shoulder. "What time is it?"

"One."

"Night or day."

"Day."

"Wow. I feel like it's still night."

"I came to tell you I have to go. I'll be gone for tonight at least. Maybe longer. Do you think you can manage?"

He smacked his lips a little. "My mouth tastes all cottony."

I handed him the water. He took it gratefully.

After he drained the whole glass, he said, "I guess I'll be all right. Mainly, I feel like I need more sleep."

"You should go easy on what you eat. There is fruit in the kitchen. You can make toast. Eggs. That sort of thing."

He nodded, his big green eyes glancing up at me, puppy-sweet. I took a half-step back at how that look made me respond. My mind retorted. *No. Just no!*

"If things get bad, is there any way I can contact you?" he asked.

"There's a burner phone right here. It's brand new." I'd risked everything to buy two of them. One I used to report in to Sam. The other I kept for Kee. "The only number in it is mine. If you text me, it will show up as anonymous." I picked up the new phone, a red flip style, and handed it to him.

"What should I say if I have to text?"

I stared at him. He really wanted me to tell him everything to do. Nice kink. I didn't tell him it was one of mine.

"Just text my name. Bast. And I mean it. It's for emergencies only. I have no time to text on my job. The boss will notice and want to know who I'm talking to."

He nodded, then winced. "Ow. My head."

"There's more aspirin on the nightstand as well. And your detox prescription, which you can have in about two hours. One pill only. Is that clear?"

"Yes, sir!" He raised his splinted hand and actually saluted me.

I frowned. "Don't do that."

"Do what?" He ducked his head and smiled, then winced again in pain.

Well fuck, this feisty street Omega was going to be the end of me.

"There's a black robe in the closet you can use. Your sleep pants have been washed and dried."

"Whatever happened to my vest and jeans?"

"I washed and dried them. The vest is fine. The jeans, what is left of them, are with it in that drawer." He pointed toward a dark dresser.

He mock-pouted. "I like jeans that are half falling apart."

"Indeed." I refrained from rolling my eyes even though the vision of him in those jeans had not left my mind since I first saw him at Moosie's.

"All right, then." I breathed out. "I'm leaving."

"Don't get yourself killed on the job. I can't do this without you," he said quickly.

Of course he needed me. For everything. I had not planned this. But it was all my fault. Now it was set in motion.

*

"Your mind is not on the job today, Sebastian," said Myre, looking up at me over his half-moon reading glasses.

I sat in a chair facing his desk with a pad in hand, going over the duty roster for everyone who worked for him beneath the veil of the casino.

Why he put me in charge of it was probably because I wasn't as goonish as his other cohorts. I had no seniority. But I could think creatively. Quickly. And I got things done while other guys were thinking with their mouths open, catching flies.

Myre noticed me from the very beginning of my employment with him and I moved up in the ranks fast enough to make Sam suspicious that the Alpha boss was onto me. That it wasn't a trap. But it turned out, Myre had few he could rely on who weren't merely henchmen or dealers or drivers. His secretary was trustworthy but lazy, always talking about the cute Omegas he'd scored with. Whereas I was more business oriented.

Sam wanted me to loosen up before this gig, play a role, but I'd quickly realized my own real personality complimented Myre's immediate needs. I was efficient, quiet and private. Soon Myre was plying me with gifts, making sure I would stay.

I got things done.

Now, with Kee in my apartment, I'd compromised everything. My mind strayed. Worried.

I glanced up. "Sir?"

"You should have had that done already. I'm counting on you."

"Almost finished." I realized I had been staring at the screen doing nothing for some minutes.

"We're all going to Albert's for dinner," Myre said.

"Required?"

"Why?" His eyebrows rose, his grizzled face smoothing out slightly, showing only a few dozen wrinkles now instead of a hundred.

I shrugged, glancing down at my screen.

"You have something better to do?"

"No, sir."

"Good, then it's settled."

But my heart beat a little faster. He'd noticed something was off. Not much got by that Alpha, which was why he was in the power position he currently held. No one had bettered Myre in decades. And no one had ever been able to take him down. He had no arrest record. He kept all his dealings under the veil, and anything illegal went through his crew. If they were caught, they alone held the bag.

Myre made sure everyone was paid well enough not to squeal. And he paid their families for insured silence if anyone did get thrown in prison. If that silence ever broke, the families would be killed.

It was simple and brilliant.

I needed to focus. I couldn't bring any attention to myself that anything in my life had changed. Kee needed to stay safe.

Because I had my own suite at the hotel, I never had anyone who worked here over to my apartment, so I didn't worry about anyone dropping by unnoticed, which was a relief.

After I finished the roster, Myre took the whole evening crew of thirteen Alphas to dinner, henchmen, drivers, everyone. He'd rented a room at the restaurant. I wondered what was so special about tonight. Myre could be generous, but always with an agenda.

He ordered the best wine, a dozen bottles over the course of the dinner. Everyone became lightly drunk and happy. The food was steak or pasta. Myre liked to see his Alphas eat hearty.

I wondered if Kee had eaten. He needed food to heal faster. He'd seemed better when I left, coherent at least, but that was no guarantee.

Again, Myre noticed my wandering attention. I was seated next to him, his right hand more and more these days, and he leaned into me and whispered, "Is your Burn coming early?"

"No, sir."

"You're thinking too hard, then. I can almost hear it."

The only true telepathy was between bond mates, so I had no fear of him. But it was odd that he sensed me so acutely.

His hand came down on the table and pressed against mine, where I leaned my weight toward the left of my practically untouched plate. I gave him a hard glance, but did not move my hand.

There had been other instances where he'd become somewhat touchy. I had brushed it off as his demeanor. But I had wondered, now and again, if he was an Alpha-lover.

He ordered beautiful Omegas right and left for the parties he threw, but I'd rarely seen him touch them. I surmised it was because he was old. An Alpha did not stop producing semen once we hit maturity and had our first Burn. But knotting might become less frequent if not vanish. Some said, with laughter in their voice, knotting was for the young. And some very old Alphas could not get hard, so even if their semen was still potent, they weren't really able to fuck.

But maybe Myre didn't like Omegas the way he pretended. All the information I had on him was mostly for the past twenty years. Current. I had no clue if he'd ever had a bond mate. Or if he had ever even had a lover.

But of course he had. What was I thinking? I'd seen him go off to private rooms with a beautiful Omega on his arm.

I didn't need to freak out.

Myre's hand was warm. His fingers pressed into mine very slightly. I took a deep, quiet breath, then said, "The wine is superb."

"Isn't it, though?" His smile crinkled his cheeks.

I had never told Sam anything in my reports about Myre's strange physical gestures toward me. They were nothing anyway. But if I knew Sam, he'd want me to run with it. He'd have had me sleeping with the old guy if it could get him this arrest, legit and secure.

I suppressed a shudder. *To the job*, my mind supplied. Well, sometimes things got more complicated than just doing one's job.

Myre never pontificated his agenda during dinner. When the meal was cleared, the doors to the private dining room opened and in trailed a crowd of beautiful, young Omegas, each one prettier than the last.

The Alphas around the table all laughed as each one grabbed a boy. Some of the boys immediately sat on laps; others hovered with their arms around their chosen Alpha.

One dark-haired beauty, much like Kee in coloring, came up behind me. Another, with silver-blond hair, approached Myre.

I allowed the Omega to fawn over me; I forced a smile. My cock even warmed a little. But I didn't want him. In truth, his hard look bored me. There was nothing behind his lovely eyes.

"I'm called Honey," he said. When he spoke, his voice sounded hollow to my ears. He had no need of me. Just *to the job.*

Like me.

"Sebastian." Myre's tone was almost cajoling. "Don't you like him?"

"Of course."

His dark look said he didn't believe me and wanted to know why. I had no reason. No reason at all, I told myself, as Kee's face flashed through my mind: his vulnerability, his pain, his defiance even when sick. He had pride. He had life in his gestures. He might have been wild and from the streets, but he kept himself well put together. Maybe it was a mask. A façade.

Yeah, I thought of him. Even when I tried hard not to. His arrogance. His need. His beauty. How the white cloth of the drawstring pants I'd loaned him turned nearly transparent when I'd thrown him in the tub, revealing strong thigh muscles and other ample endowments. I couldn't stop seeing the image of him, naked before me, when I'd peeled that wet cloth away from his skin and put him to bed.

Honey hung on my arm for the rest of the evening until the late hour broke us all up and all the Alphas went to their cars arm in arm with their Omegas, taking them home for some more fun.

92

Myre watched me on and off the whole night. My entire body remained tense as I tried to guess if he suspected me of something, or if he simply wanted to make sure I had a good time.

I had driven to dinner with Myre. When we all returned to his car, the Omegas came, too. Once we got back to the hotel, Myre parted ways with me in the hall.

"Have a good evening." He winked. His gaze lingered on me a little too long.

He expected me to take Honey with me to my suite, when all I could think of was getting home to check on Kee.

"You have a suite here, too?" Honey asked me.

"Yes."

If I didn't take Honey with me, Myre would see. So I grasped his hand and walked him down the hall.

Once in the suite, Honey shrieked with pleasure at the luxuries: the big bed, the glass ornaments on every surface, the crystal lamps and chandelier, private kitchen, hot tub bath.

My mind started creating all manner of excuses for me to get out of this. It was not an uncommon situation; it had happened before and it was going to be happening again and again.

I could tell Myre I had an exclusive lover, but then Myre would want to meet him. I could claim sudden illness. But then Myre would want to check on me, and wonder why I didn't stay in the suite where I would have everything catered to me.

Sam had always told me to keep things simple. If he were standing before me, he would recommend I sleep with Honey, then dismiss him, and go on about my life as usual.

But Honey, for all his beauty and sweetness, did not intrigue me, and I had no arousal for him. Non-arousal would be considered odd by my peers, and grounds for suspicion that something wasn't right with me, but they didn't have to know. At least not this time.

I approached Honey with a handful of bills. "Stay the night. Do what you wish. Sleep. Eat. Take a long bath in the hot tub."

Honey pouted. "But you're not staying?"

"I have a Burn coming on," I lied. "I already paid for a farm Omega. If I start with you, I won't stop and Myre paid for you only for tonight, yes?"

"Yes."

"You're quite beautiful, and I would never normally turn down a gift so precious from the boss, which is why I would ask you, as a favor only, to not mention it to him that we didn't spend the night together."

"Of course, sir." He smiled. "Thank you for letting me stay."

I believed he was earnest. But he might blab later on about this evening. About my behavior.

I was taking risks Sam would never approve. In fact, if he knew about any of the things I'd done in the past week, he'd possibly pull me from the field. But I couldn't have that. Not when we were so close to building the case against Myre.

I wouldn't be able to live with myself if I were responsible for letting Myre get away with everything he'd done not just during the two years I'd worked for him, but for decades.

I slipped out of the suite and down the hall. This time there was no guard on the elevator because we didn't have any current prisoners. There was no danger. Everything was locked down tight.

The cameras might catch me making my escape, but Myre wouldn't look at the footage if he saw no need. Still, I made sure I kept to the known blind spots as I made my way to the parking garage and my car.

It was nearly eleven-thirty when I pulled into my parking space in front of my apartment. When I walked through my front door, I was immediately greeted by a beautiful Omega in a black robe twirling and spinning about the room. The TV

94

blared some sort of music noise, an assault on the ears, actually, and the hem of the robe flew outward revealing strong, gold thighs and the hint of a tight, curvy rear.

I needn't have worried after all.

"You're feeling better I see," I said, stepping through the door, closing and locking it behind me.

Kee jumped back, his mouth opening, and let out a shocked yell that sounded something like "what" and "oh" combined into a single inarticulate word.

"Bast! Fuck, I didn't hear you!"

I wanted to smile. Instead, I strode to coffee the table, picked up the remote and turned down the volume on the TV.

I looked him over, toes to forehead. "No more cramps? Fever? Headache? And your toe must not be hurting much anymore."

"I had some cramps earlier in the day. I slept more and when I woke I was starving. After I ate, I suddenly had all this energy."

I hoped it wasn't simply a bout of withdrawal-hyperactivity, his body reacting to a different sort of high as all the toxins made their final exit from his body. But when I remembered Kee from the club, how energized he was to look at, how he commanded all those around him with little effort, I decided this was the real deal.

Kee's personality was obviously based on moving all the time, pleasure, indulgence, filling the room with his charisma. He thrived on activity, not inertia. He focused on what made him feel good in the moment.

"The goal is to keep you hidden, to maintain your presence here as a secret," I said.

"The curtains are closed. No one can see in," he retorted.

I let out a deep breath. "I could hear the loud music from the parking lot."

"So?"

"It brings attention to this apartment. To you."

"What? Your neighbors? It's none of their business."

"It is if they call the cops."

He bowed his head. "I wasn't *that* loud."

"The fact is, I am never loud. They aren't used to this noise coming from my apartment."

He raised his head, his green eyes squinting as if he were deep in thought. "Like you can't have a guest?"

He was right in that observation. Of course I could have guests. In the past two years I'd been around mostly to sleep. I didn't know my neighbors and they did not know me. Still, I didn't want to take any unnecessary chances.

"This is serious, Kee." If anything happened to him, I didn't know what I'd do.

"I know it is."

"Just don't do anything stupid. And keep those curtains closed."

He stood in the middle of the living room in my short black robe, arms wrapped around his chest, and solemnly nodded.

Chapter Eleven

Kee

Keep the volume low. Keep the curtains closed. Don't do anything stupid.

I couldn't quite tell if Bast was worried or angry or both because he always wore that look on his face of utter distaste, as if he'd just eaten something sour and couldn't wash the flavor away.

Don't do anything stupid. Was that what he thought of me? That I was a stupid Omega who had no sense? No survival instinct? For a moment, I was livid and hurt and defensive.

I wanted to tell him I'd survived the Trenches longer than most who started out young. I wanted to tell him my Omega father had been strong but poor only because of insane laws that kept Omegas from getting good paying jobs or keeping their own bank accounts without an Alpha guardian.

I had learned to live on cash only. I paid as I went. I had no debt. I sold my body because it was what I had to offer, and because I was good at sex. Staying on the streets certainly shortened my lifespan, and I was perfectly aware of that. I hadn't planned to live past thirty anyway.

"I'm trying to keep you alive," Bast said, shrugging out of his jacket and hanging it on a hook by the door.

"It's not like I got snagged by your boss on purpose," I said. "He believes something about me that isn't true. I have no control over that."

Bast's eyebrows rose in question. The muscles of his face hardened. "I'm not saying it is your fault that you're here."

"Whose fault is it? Why does Myre think I did anything to cause his beloved men—who are criminals, by the way—to be arrested?"

"Street gossip."

"Does he usually get his intelligence in that manner?"

Bast turned away and moved toward the kitchen. "Have you eaten?"

"Who influences him? You're pretty close to him, right? Did you hear gossip about me? Did you go along with his ridiculous and paranoid conclusions about a street Omega who only likes to party a little hard?"

Bast had his back to me when he answered. "I suggested maybe his cousin and friend were loud, and if they drank a lot—which they always did—they might have a tendency to brag to their bed partners."

Bast's shoulders went taut. He gave a tiny jerk of his head which, if I hadn't been looking right at him, I would have missed. The tells were obvious. Bast thought he was to blame for my predicament.

"I didn't even know you. In Moosie's that night, that was the first time I ever saw you," I said.

"Yes. I didn't know your name. Others did. By reputation alone, you were convicted."

"But you believe me, right? That I didn't tell any cops a thing about anyone, not your boss, or who sold me steam on any given night. Nothing. I don't rat on people."

"Yes."

"Yes, what?"

The tight shoulders went back even further, causing a crease down the spine of his perfect, black shirt. He wouldn't face me. "Yes. I believe you."

It was as if air came into me, lifting a heaviness from my body which I'd felt ever since Myre had kidnapped me. I couldn't figure out why it was so important to me that Bast believe me. Believe *in* me. But there it was. That strange need for someone to know my truth. And to not condemn me just because they saw Omega gutter trash, a no good soon to be washed-up whore.

"I know I'm trash, but there is still some honor in the streets."

Bast turned half toward me, the kitchen light outlining his black-clad form in pale blue. "I never thought you were trash."

I put my hands on my hips. "Why not? Everyone does. Alphas most especially."

"Most Omegas are raised to rent their bodies."

"Yeah, but most operate under established businesses. Farms, cloister homes, clubs and brothels. Most aren't fucked up addicts."

He turned and contemplated me, his brow smooth now, his lips slightly parted. He was beautiful when he wasn't trying to be all tough and hard-assed. "The laws in place prohibit you from moving forward. That does not make you trash."

"I had a chance to move forward once. An Alpha. Willing to teach me. To sponsor me." I bowed my head at my memories with Tarin. One of the good ones.

Bast swung his hands behind his back. "Yes, all those messages from a single source on your phone. Tarin. You mentioned him."

"Yes. And I chose the gutter instead. I chose my freedom and my stupid life and my steam."

How did this happen? Suddenly, the conversation was getting far too personal.

Bast blinked twice, slowly. "I'm sure you had your reasons."

"My reason for steam is that I like it." My face heated. "I like being high."

He took a breath. Opened his mouth. Closed it. And ended up saying nothing.

The silence grated. "It's easier," I said, filling the room with my voice. "Easier than reality. Easier than thinking about being a waste of space, of breath, of other people's time."

He continued to assess me with that unnerving stare.

I continued. "I don't like being alone." My voice hitched. I went to the couch and sat down hard. "That's why I had the TV on so loud. Why I was spinning around the room. That's a natural high." I felt my lips curve up a bit. "I hate being alone."

"I'm doing my best." His tone softened. I almost didn't hear the way he took a breath between his sentences. "There's no other way right now. No one we can trust."

"It's all right." I leaned my head all the way back on the couch until my hair touched the curtains behind it, and blinked away a sting in my eyes. "I'm a big boy. I'll manage."

It was certainly ironic that thugs had tried to kill me and now I was hiding in a thug's home. Well, apartment, actually. It barely looked lived in. He'd done so much for me, though. How could I ask for more?

But it sucked that now Bast was home, it was already night. He'd sleep and leave again in the morning. I'd sleep and wake alone for tomorrow. And the next day and the next.

Suddenly, I didn't feel well. Again. My eyes ached with tiredness, though I'd done almost nothing all day. Getting up and dancing around the room had gotten my energy going, but now I was depleted again.

I didn't move and in my current position could not see Bast. I heard him go into the kitchen. Rustling. Then nothing.

Spoken words broke into my doze. "Here is tea if you want it."

I lifted my head and saw Bast set a steaming mug of tea on the coffee table in front of me.

I leaned forward and took the mug. It nearly burned my hand so I grasped the handle and blew on the surface of the hot liquid.

Bast sat in a chair beside the couch. The TV still flickered before us in mute mode. It was a strange and weirdly intimate setting. An Alpha and an Omega sharing mugs of tea close to midnight with no words between them.

The tea was wonderful, sweetened just the way I liked. I rarely made tea for myself. I was a coffee drinker, and I snatched cups, in-between bouts of partying, as often as possible.

We each finished our drink without a word, our eyes hypnotically drawn to the silent TV. I realized when I set down my mug that technically I was in Bast's bed. The couch was where he'd slept the rare nights he was here.

My body still felt depleted but the tea had quieted my roiling stomach. I stood, stretching my arms over my head, only realizing too late that I made the robe slide all the way up my upper thighs.

I glanced at Bast, feeling that dark-eyed gaze almost like fingers tracing up and down my bare legs. I watched him dart his glance away, watched the darkening of his cheeks and all those little telltale signs of emotion he would not overtly show. But to me, his feelings were clear and expressive, even if subtle on the outside.

It was almost as if I could feel the surging of his blood. The frustration behind having me here, an unanticipated guest who took his bed and not only that, was Omega gutter trash to boot. I almost heard his inner grumble, his war inside that was about his responsibility toward me and his own peril all of that brought.

"I'm exhausted. Good night," I said.

He sat with his hands locked around his now empty mug, staring off, gazing anywhere but at me.

I wanted to think he was not repelled by me, but attracted. But that didn't seem likely. Bast worked for a hard man of an elite killer gang that ran most of the city's underground businesses. He wasn't the least bit romantic about it or about saving me, but all business as usual.

As I got into bed and under the covers, I saw him again and again in my mind. His sharp, stony face, his unique stillness and silence even when he moved, even when he spoke, words clipped and circumspect. He did not participate in idle chit-chat. He was probably the most impeccable Alpha I'd ever met, which was both a compliment and a disappointment, since he appeared impossible to reach.

Yet, he'd bathed me when I was feverish. He'd sat by my bedside when I was the sickest and most in need. He'd shown an odd loyalty to my well-being.

He was so unlike Tarin, who wanted to do things for me but have me love him in return. Tarin who wore his emotions for me on his sleeve, who held so tight sometimes I needed to run just to feel I could breathe again.

Bast wasn't like that. Did I want him to be?

And I still kept wondering why in all the combined hells he saved my life.

I turned onto my side, clutching a balled up pillow. I shut my eyes so tight I saw white at the edges of my blanked out vision, then held my breath as I allowed my next thought to wash over me.

Maybe I was the one attracted to Bast.

Therein lay all my problems. My confusions and indecisions. When I confronted the realization head on, my cock twitched. My ass clenched. I bit my lower lip, realizing it was true. The bodily response made it official.

Sure, I'd had lots of sex, but that didn't mean I was attracted to the Alphas I did business with. Business was business. Bast was anything but.

At long last it had happened. There was an Alpha I wanted who didn't want me back.

Frustrated, I tossed and turned in the bed, waking in the early morning hours covered in sweat. I'd had terrible fever dreams all night but they faded quickly until I couldn't remember them.

I got up and took a quick, cool shower.

When I came into the living room, Bast was already up and preparing breakfast. I sat at the kitchen table and watched him, secretly hoping he'd made enough for two.

Wordlessly, he set a plate of scrambled eggs and bacon and toast in front of me.

"Will you be back tonight?" I asked.

"I never know from one day to the next. Often Myre will have me on call, which means I stay in my suite."

"Is it really your suite?" I asked.

"It's a guest suite. But Myre never lets anyone else use it."

"He gave it to you."

Bast nodded, sitting down across from me with his own plate of food.

"He likes you." I took a bite of toast. "How old is he?"

Bast stopped in mid-chew, frowning. "I don't know."

"He looks about two hundred at least."

"Hmm." Bast continued to eat, not looking at me.

"I wonder if he's been a murderer his whole life. That's a long time. A lot of bodies."

Bast swallowed hard, glancing up. That dark-dark look again. My cock actually twitched. It usually had somewhat better judgment. While I'd sleep with any Alpha who paid well, my cock showed interest in only a few. This Alpha worked for a killer, which by default made him one, too.

"Do you ever get tired of it? This life?"

"I don't know what you mean." Bast sat back and took a drink of orange juice.

Of course he would say that. He could have asked the same question of me. And the answer would have been no. At least at first. It was my defensive retort, to always say I did what I wanted. I loved my life and I had better live it up because it would be a short one anyway.

Truth was, I didn't want to die. I simply saw no alternative lifestyle to embrace. It always seemed I was too late for everything and anything.

"My father always used to say you aren't what you do. That means you do a certain job to survive, but it doesn't have to define who you are."

"I know what it means," Bast replied. "The actual quote is your job is not you. It's from fifty years ago. The famous psychologist Doctor Yurbo."

"It's because people find themselves in shit situations. Getting out might be impossible for a while, or forever."

"If you're implying my situation is shit—"

I held my hand up. "I was implying mine is."

Bast scooped up more eggs onto his last piece of toast and downed it in a single bite. He stood, taking his plate to the sink.

"I'll do the dishes," I offered. It was the least I could do. I was contributing nothing here but breathing, and even that was taking air, not giving anything back.

"You know the emergency text number. I will try to come home tonight but no guarantees."

I wanted to salute him. *Yes, sir!* But I stayed seated at the table and watched him walk into the living room. He gathered his keys, wallet and coat and the last I saw of him was the hem of his long coat flailing behind him, almost getting caught in the door as it shut.

*

Bast did not come home that night. Or the next. And he sent me zero texts.

There was only so much TV a person could watch before they got a bit antsy. I'd slept a lot. The withdrawal was still happening in my body but at least I was eating again. When I wasn't getting the shakes or feeling too hot, I felt excessive amounts of energy, as if it all built up in me at once about to explode.

I put on the TV to a music channel I liked, a bit lower in the volume since the first time I did it, and danced around the entire place, jumping on the couch, the coffee table, the chair where Bast last sat drinking tea. I would run into the bedroom and jump on the bed. When I got tired, I dragged myself back into the living room and flopped on the couch.

Sometimes I parted the curtains and peered out, my heart pounding in my throat. Bast had put a good and solid fear in me. I had the weird fantasy that every time I looked out I'd see a wrinkled, desert-wracked two-hundred year old face peering back at me.

If I were found, what would I do? I'd try to run, of course.

But no faces peered at me. No one seemed to notice I was even here in this silent, un-warm apartment. The front of the complex was green grass and dusty-looking bushes. The parking lot was nearly empty. This was the sort of place where people who weren't rich lived. They worked every day just to pay the rent. I could feel it all around me. The other apartments were mostly empty during the day.

The sun shone on a scattering of golden leaves from several trees lining the asphalt lot. It looked warm and inviting. I was a night person, for sure, but during the days when I woke late, wherever I was I often tried to find a patio and a lounge to occupy while nursing my hangovers from the previous evening. I loved feeling the warm light on my skin and in my hair. I luxuriated in the natural heat that embraced the Earth.

Now here I was behind thick curtains cooped up, bored, still craving steam in my darker hours, and there was nothing I could do about it.

Then I remembered: Bast had a tiny porch or patio out the back kitchen door. That door was double locked, with a bolt lock and a hinge clamp. Like he never used it, never went out that way. But I'd had a peek through the back door window and seen the little concrete area surrounded by a wrought-iron railing. It was a place a person would put potted plants and maybe even a barbeque grill if they actually spent time in the apartment. If they actually had a life.

I unlocked both extra locks and the door lock itself, then opened the door onto fresh sweet air and sunshine. I stepped out onto the barren patio area and breathed in deep. The scent of fresh mowed grass filled me up. The view was a small grassy field with a few trees and bushes and a concrete path winding its way to another apartment building, but part of the same complex. Everything looked neat and tidy, fresh and clean.

I wanted to drag a chair out here and sit for a while. It was so peaceful. So calming. For a moment I rested my hands on the wrought-iron fence, the coolness seeping into my palms. I breathed in and out, realizing little moans of pleasure escaped my throat as I did so.

No one was around. The apartments just across the way had their curtains well-drawn. I felt safe. Relaxed. For the moment, I was in no pain. My finger was splinted and secure, and as long as nothing touched the top of my toe, like socks or shoes, it was also fine. I gave a little spin and felt my mouth break into a grin. I had so much energy I wanted to fun forever into that sunshine and soft green carpet of lawn.

"Hello."

My whole body jerked in shock. I turned around and saw no one.

"Up here. I live one story up."

I glanced above me at all the balconies within sight and saw a man on the balcony above and to my right. I'd completely missed him! My heart went into my throat.

He had blond curls sticking out in all directions, a sweet smile, and his slender body was clad in pink shorts and a blue-striped shirt. An Omega.

His balcony wasn't empty. It had tons of potted plants—flowers, ivy, big leafed clusters—and there was, indeed, a grill off to the side for cooking. Chimes hung from the roof eaves, glinting silver and gold in the sunlight.

"Sorry. Didn't mean to startle you," he said in a pleasant voice.

I gulped hard. In that moment, my mind played every scenario. He was a spy. He was one of Myre's crew's Omegas, I surmised, even though Bast had said he lived far away from anything work-related. He would tell the world I was here.

"I'm Del. What's your name?"

"Tarin," I lied. It was the first name I could come up with. An Alpha name. The Alpha who I'd known from the past.

"Nice to meet you, Tarin. Did you just move in here with your Alpha?"

I nodded mutely, realizing I was still wearing only the short black robe Bast had loaned me.

"It's a lovely day, isn't it?" Del said.

I took a deep breath. He was harmless. Why should I be scared? Bast had things handled on his end. This was merely a neighbor who knew nothing about me, who was simply being friendly. If I ignored him, I'd look strange. I'd bring attention to myself.

"It is lovely," I replied. "And it is very nice to meet you, too."

Del had a big smile with shiny white teeth. His golden hair curled all over the place, some locks were like corkscrews sticking out. "I'm watering my plants. And thinking maybe I'll grill some chicken out here for dinner for me and my Alpha husband."

"Oh. Wow. You're married. That's great!"

"Oh, aren't you?"

I shook my head.

"Maybe soon?" Del offered.

I gave him a big sigh with one of my goofiest grins. "We'll see, right?"

"But you're living together, so that's a plus."

"For now." I thought about what a laugh Bast would have over this conversation. If, indeed, he ever laughed.

"My Alpha and I have been bond mates since we met at the Farm in the Mating Hall. I'll never forget. As soon as I walked in the room I knew instantly this was my mate. He says he knew, too."

A little jealousy flashed through me. "That's great."

"I'll admit, a part of me never believed in the fated mates myth. It's romantic fiction. That's what I believed. But then I saw Kyto. And I just knew. He had a look when he saw me, too. I was so glad it wasn't one-sided. Wouldn't that have been a tragedy!"

"It would have," I agreed.

"Kyto works for the planning department. Low level management right now, but he's climbing that corporate ladder. We'll be out of this complex and into our own house probably by next year."

"That's great news!" I meant it. Sort of. This Omega in the pink shorts sure liked to talk.

"You're welcome to come over any time for a glass of wine. We can gossip a bit. I can fill you in on all the Omegas who live in the complex."

"Thank you. Maybe some time."

"But not today?" Del had the audacity to look disappointed. And we didn't even know each other.

"Can't right now. I have plans," I lied.

"That's cool."

Suddenly, I heard the front door open. Every part of me froze for a moment. I quickly shook that off and said, "Hey, gotta go right now. Later!"

I backed quickly into the kitchen, but not quickly enough.

Bast strode toward me, eyeing the open door. He grabbed my upper arm and yanked me back. "What are you doing?"

Still holding onto me, he shut and locked the door with his free hand, then spun about to glare at me.

I tried to pull out of his grasp but he had me in a firm grip. The black robe was already short. As he held my arm at a weird angle, the thin satiny material rode up.

I shouldn't have cared. I didn't. Not really. But this was Bast who was a gangster, a no-nonsense sort of Alpha, and the guy who'd saved my life. And I felt completely exposed. I

108

wasn't usually intimidated by Alphas. Not usually concerned with their opinions, either, except pertaining to my attractiveness, and whether they wanted me or not. It was my bottom line. Luring them and getting paid.

This was different. I felt at once guilty, ashamed, defensive and angry. His fingers on my arm were hurting me. On purpose. He was furious.

I gave a growl and again tried to spin away. It didn't work. "I was getting some fresh air. Gods!"

He yanked me again, but he must have seen something cross my face because he dropped my arm right away. "You were talking to someone!"

"Just an Omega. He lives next door and one flight up."

Bast shook his head. "I can't believe it. I told you not to speak to anyone. No one can know you're here!"

He was right, of course. I stomped my foot like a child. "I know! I know it! But I've been cooped up here for days. I only went on the little porch for a breath of fresh air. I didn't see anyone around. I thought it would be safe."

"You thought? You?"

I blinked at him. So he did think me stupid. He looked me up and down. My skin tingled as if it could feel the pressure of his gaze.

"You aren't even dressed!"

I opened my mouth to make a retort, but nothing came out. I backed up and the backs of my knees hit a kitchen chair. I sat, gazing up at him. Then I lowered my head. "I'm sorry."

"Don't. Just don't."

Bast went to the cupboard and started throwing things on the counter. Food items. He was going to prepare a meal.

"I already ate," I said softly.

"That's fine. I'm hungry, though." He was terse. Cold.

He set about making toasted cheese sandwiches. One of my favorite foods.

"Actually, I could eat," I said. Keeping my tone flat.

He refused to answer me, but I saw him making three of them. I assumed it would be one for me, two for him.

My stomach rumbled at the odors from the fried bread and melting cheese.

When he was done, he took out two plates. He put one sandwich on each plate and cut the other in half, placing one half on each plate. Then he turned and held out one plate to me.

I took it, watching as he took his and without a backward glance, went into the living room. I followed.

Bast sat in his usual chair, a beer in hand. I had my plate and a bottle of water I'd left on the coffee table. Bast used the remote to turn on the TV. He never looked at me. He ate slowly, chewing methodically, his eyes intent on the TV screen.

The air was awkward between us. Tense. He hated me, I was sure of it. I'd fucked up.

Why, then, was I so very very aroused?

Chapter Twelve

Bast

I sat in the chair by the couch with my beer, still fuming over catching Kee talking to a neighbor.

For two days Myre had kept me on call. Most of that time he spent with me, sometimes alone, sometimes with others.

It happened sometimes. Myre liked having me around. Said I had a brain and it was refreshing after dealing all day with *animals.*

He took me to fancy lunches and dinners. In his limo, in the backseat, he touched me often as he spoke. On the hand. On the forearm. A couple of times on the thigh.

It had taken a long time for Myre to trust me, even though I'd moved up fast in the ranks. Tonight, he'd caught my eye with his gaze more and more, as if sharing some secret. Once he said, "It's you and me against the world now. You know that, right?"

Sam would have been ecstatic. Seduce him more, would have been Sam's pronouncement.

But Myre was smarter than anyone had given him credit for two years ago when I'd been sent to infiltrate his organization. I could be standing right next to him when he texted a hit on someone with an untraceable phone, and never know it. This was because he had code words for his orders. And each person working for him seemed to have a different code, a different understanding of what he wanted. Darker deeds could be passed from person to person until the string of commands was so long the initial order was almost insignificant. Myre might defend himself by saying he had not ordered any hit but had only been speaking in anger, or joking.

Myre had people who had people who did things for him. Including record-keeping and finances. He had legit businesses the law could not find fault with. It had been impossible to touch him. Until I came along.

I had badly wanted to check in on Kee. But Myre had kept me on call for two nights straight. He came into my suite early to have breakfast with me, and kept me late in his own penthouse suite, insisting I watch his action movies with him on his huge wall-screen TV and drink his expensive whiskey.

Over two days had passed by the time I was able to drive away and go home. Not that my apartment was any real home. But I kept it just the same. And with Kee there now, I had someone other than Sam or Myre relying on me. Someone who also needed looking after. Someone who had been innocent and almost died on my watch.

It was a strange feeling for me to actually look forward to going home. Before Kee, I mostly stayed at the hotel. I went to my apartment when I really needed to get away from everything, and to sleep without being on call.

I couldn't rationalize in my mind that I actually wanted to see Kee. I told myself I was merely concerned for his safety. The last time I'd come in on him dancing to the TV turned on high volume. This night, as I drove home, I'd been curious what I would find. The Omega was the sort who could too easily get himself in trouble. But I was fairly confident I'd communicated to him the real sort of danger he was in. He had to realize it. He had come very close to being killed and never seen or heard from again.

I also worried his withdrawal from steam had not been complete. Was he sick and needed my help? Had I stayed away too long?

I'd driven a bit faster as images of him lying ill and helpless on my bathroom floor peppered my mind.

When I entered the living room it had been quiet and empty. This time no TV blared in my face. No Kee bouncing around the room with his robe flying up revealing a bit too much skin.

I'd glanced in the bedroom through the open door only to see it was empty. Then I'd heard voices coming from the kitchen.

Voices plural?

No! He couldn't have invited anyone into the apartment. He certainly knew better than that.

I'd entered the kitchen to see the outer door to the back patio was open. I'd seen Kee standing, still in the black robe and gazing upward. Someone was talking to him.

Kee had turned to see me and quickly backed into the kitchen.

I'd panicked and grabbed his arm just as he turned to see me.

I'd yanked him into the kitchen. I'd never had such fear and fury in my life, not when I was proving myself to Myre by doing despicable things, not even when I'd left him all alone in the forest by his empty grave.

All I could see in that moment were enemies everywhere, all with their eyes trained on Kee.

I didn't remember what I said to him that night. Not exactly. But his beautiful green eyes popped wide as we'd faced each other off in the kitchen. He'd said something about an Omega neighbor. He'd apologized. None of it was enough.

I'd fixed a light dinner and ate it, still fuming, furious. Scared to death for both our lives. A simple mistake was all it took to ruin my cover, to make us both targets who would never escape the long reach of Myre.

Now, the long silence grew between us. The TV was like a buffer, but it didn't correct the problem. I couldn't see or hear it. I couldn't taste my food as I ate.

Kee sat picking at his sandwich, then eating it as if he were commanded, without feeling. One program ended. Another began. It was early yet. Not even dark outside.

Kee moved his knee up and down. He set his plate on the coffee table. He tapped his fingers—the unbroken ones—against his chest, then his thigh, then a pillow.

The air in the room felt explosive. The tension could be tasted—like salt and rust combined.

Finally, Kee spoke. "I was worried about you being gone so long. I'm glad you're back."

"I am at Myre's beck and call. There are no set hours. I told you that."

"I know." He lifted his head but continued to stare at the TV

I turned to really look at him now, assess him. Finally able to focus without the glaze of my anger, my fear.

His hair was bright today, and neatly brushed back. His skin glowed. He looked better than when I'd left him, not sick anymore, not hung over from withdrawal. Again, the fresh peach scent wafted off him, brushing over my skin as if scent could actually touch like hands and fingers. I felt my mouth water. There was no doubt this Omega was beguiling, but I usually had more control about such matters.

My cock gave a gentle throb. My heartbeat increased.

Kee's features in profile were regal, strong. He easily could have passed for an Alpha if not for his scent. He had unusual height for an Omega, and the muscle on him had been worked at. I liked that about him. He wasn't weak or fawning. At least not in my presence. Maybe he behaved that way toward clients who expected it, but I wasn't a client. He'd made me an offer only once, and that was when he was at his worst, wanting an exchange for drugs.

But he was trouble for himself. He was a wild card. Myre would have dismissed him as untrustworthy if he'd had him on his crew, if Kee had been an Alpha. It was because Kee was wily, which made his nature unpredictable.

Kee needed stability. I could give it. Maybe. But I wasn't around enough. But maybe if I set out tasks for him. Discipline.

At the word *discipline*, my cock gave another twitch.

It was ridiculous to think Kee would respond in any manner to what I wanted for him. To keep him safe first and foremost. But more?

I couldn't think it.

He was wild. His restlessness put him in danger. If he wouldn't listen to me…

But could I make him?

Before I could squash that thought, my body became very intrigued at the idea. *No*, I told myself. *Just no*. He was very attractive. That was all this was. My crazy ideas for more intimacy were just that. Nuts. And stemming from no other fact than that Kee needed to stay safe.

As for the discipline part—meaning tasks and chores—I had to try. It would keep him occupied, at least. Avoid boredom.

"What do you think about pale blue for this room?" I asked calmly, as if we'd been conversing easily since we sat down.

"What?"

"I've been thinking of repainting the living room."

"Oh! Um. Pale blue would be better for the bedroom." He shook his head as if to get himself out of some distant headspace, and glanced up, then right to left. He pointed to the wall by the door. "Off-white on that one maybe. Then maybe pale gold?"

His quick suggestion had me raising my eyebrows. "Really?"

"I saw a two-tone room like it once. It was very nice."

"I'll bring some paint chips in. You can choose."

Kee tilted his head. "When will you have the time to paint?"

"Most likely, I won't."

"You want me to…?"

"If you'd like."

"Yes!" He sat up straighter. "I mean, okay. It's fine. I think it would be fun." He gazed around the room again. "I'll

115

have to move things. I'll have to have a lot of brushes and drop cloths and stuff."

"I will get them or make sure they are delivered." Maybe it would keep him too busy to make more friends of the neighbors.

"I am sorry about Del." Kee took a deep breath.

"Del?" The name did not register.

"The Omega next door. I really didn't mean to talk to him. He doesn't know who I am. At all."

But he might know me through others in the complex. I didn't have friends here, though I'd lived in the apartment for two years. My name was known to the manager who collected the rent. Managers got around. And managers talked. I mailed in my rent, but others waited until the last minute, or paid late, and therefore went to the manager in person. It was impossible to have an apartment complex where people didn't talk about the other tenants.

Feeling better about the future, now that I'd come up with a task for Kee, I had a pretty good night on the couch, aside from my dreams. Dreams of Kee in the bedroom and me sleeping next to him breathing in his peach scent. Of Kee naked, hair tumbled, clinging to me, bending for me, his muscular buttocks practically in my face, giving me his cat's eye looks over his shoulder as he drew me in and in and in.

*

"You are not like the others," Myre said.

Two days had passed, and again Myre had kept me from going home. Kept me from Kee.

I saved and filed the reports he'd asked me to look over. Paperwork on money I'd collected earlier in the day. It had gone smoothly except for one hardhead. I'd had to get a bit physical there, and it had left a raw taste in me, as well as a hyped up energy.

116

I sat at Myre's second computer at a typing desk about six feet away from his desk. Fresh flowers scented the room. Lilies. He had them delivered every day from a florist shop he controlled in the busiest part of the city. He laundered money there, and I had proof, but that wasn't big enough for Sam to make an arrest.

Sam wanted to get Myre for life, even though no one knew how many years he had left. The average Alpha lifespan was two hundred years. Myre looked at least one-ninety-nine.

Now I glanced up.

Myre was giving me one of his discomforting stares again. Like he wanted to eat me or fuck me. Or both.

After two years, and Myre now treating me like some old friend, I still had only brief insights into what made him tick. I'd seen him go off with pretty Omegas almost nightly, but I'd heard on the rumor mill he didn't fuck them. He made them do things. Play. Sometimes he had two or three. I believe they put on shows. Beyond that, I tried not to think about it. I didn't want to know what Myre did behind closed doors. Although lately, it appeared as if he wanted to know what I did. He was more and more curious. Asking me questions he'd never asked in two years. Private questions I tried to avoid and deflect, such as:

"Do you prefer blonds or brunets?"

"Don't you have a Burn coming? Go on and take a few days off. If you need my help procuring an Omega to your tastes, you need only ask."

"Have you ever had two at once? It's marvelous. Ah, to be young again!"

Myre never asked anything without an agenda. These were subtle ways of finding out more information about me. About my personal habits and lifestyle. I gave vague and probably unsatisfactory answers, but he merely smiled, the skin of his face breaking into dozens of more wrinkles. Then he would surprise me with a set of gold cufflinks, or a fancy pen in a satin case.

"For a job well-done. You saved me money," he would always say.

And several times, it was true. I'd caught accounting errors that showed his guy was not the best at his job. I'd brought other problematic concerns to his attention, which he fixed in his own ways. He either got rid of the problem, which meant it was probably six feet under, or he switched employees around, changing shifts, hiring more spies.

"Tonight, I have something special planned. I want you to come with me," Myre said. His eyes were like hard, dark crystals. The look in them said, *You cannot refuse.*

When the day ended, Myre took me to one of the hotel's most elegant, private dining rooms. All I could think about was when I'd get home, and what I'd find Kee up to. He'd been painting for days. He had finished the living room and wanted to tackle the bedroom.

I was relieved to see him keep busy, but also taken with his attention to detail, his color choices, his ability to do such a perfect job while still healing from a broken finger.

Though I had ordered him some clothes, he wore his torn up jeans to paint in. And nothing else. They were threadbare, a stone-washed blue with bleached white seams that hugged his ass in unbelievable tightness. Little rips exposed his upper thighs, nearly revealing the lower parts of both cheeks. Walking in the front door and seeing him like that, his hair tied back in a messy tail, his muscles moving under his honey-dark skin as he moved the roller back and forth, had me breathless. And I did not get breathless. Not ever. I held control and prided myself on it.

Kee turned everything upside-down.

Myre ordered the most expensive wine. We did not have menus, so he'd planned the dinner ahead of time. I was uncomfortable with the fact that no one else had been invited.

Myre started out talking casually about the week. He rarely made small talk, but when he asked me, "Do you think it might rain?" I was taken off guard.

118

I nodded. "The weather calls for a storm tonight."

"I love storms. Their power. Their beauty. The mood of them goes straight to here." He thumped himself on his chest. "The best is when a storm correlates perfectly with the Burn. Ah, the energy intensifies."

Did Myre still even have Burns? I couldn't be sure.

"You have a Burn coming up, don't you?"

I let out a slow breath through my nose. Myre made it his business to know my schedule, down to the wire, and that of most of his employees. He did not like to be caught off-guard or surprised if someone couldn't make it to work due to that damned feverish need to procreate.

"I do."

"Another week, correct?"

My face heated a little. "Correct."

I'd already made plans to go to a chattel farm. My Burns were short. Myre would miss me for a day at most. I would not mention it at all to Kee.

Suddenly, Myre made a confession I had never expected. "I miss them."

"Sir?"

"Burns."

I pressed my lips hard together, wondering what I should say.

"You look uncomfortable," he accused with a slash of a smile. "The subject bother you? My men talk about it all the time. Brag, actually."

I nodded. "Yes. They do."

"But not you. Why?"

I started to protest.

Myre held his hand up to stop me. "You're very private. I know. If I were a more paranoid man, I might think you were up to something."

My heart revved up.

"But," he continued softer, his voice almost praising. "You're more a cerebral man. I appreciate that." His smile widened to a grimace. "But when you let loose, I'll bet you are wild." He let out a terrible laugh.

I glanced away, grabbing my glass of wine and taking a long sip.

"Do you have anyone steady?" Myre asked me.

"No."

"I didn't think so. I ask only because I smell Omega on you. And you rarely have anyone at your suite. I've checked."

I looked him directly in the eyes then. "You checked?"

"I did. You don't mind, do you? You know I keep you closest to me in my activities so I like to know what you're doing."

All the time? I wondered.

"So then you must partake outside the hotel. Other times. At your apartment."

Thinking quickly, I lied. "The scent on me you smell. Uh, well, I have an Alpha neighbor. Sometimes I go over for barbecues. He has an Omega husband and two children. One is an Omega."

"Ah. I see. Yes. That might be it."

The way he said *might* told me he did not believe me. If he spied on me all the time, did that mean he spied at my apartment? I knew Kee kept the curtains closed all the time now. He was good about that. But he had accepted deliveries. Paint. Painting accessories. New clothes. Some grocery drop-offs. I realized I had not been as strict as I should have about that sort of thing.

A sudden fear settled in me that Kee was in danger. Perhaps at this very moment. It wasn't the fact that I had an Omega staying with me. It was the fact that he was Kee. And Kee was supposed to be dead.

"Don't look so worried," Myre said. He let out a strange laugh again. "I only wondered if you ever take outside partners into your Burns."

"What do you mean *outside*?"

"If you, for example, might share an Omega with another Alpha." He paused, his eyelids closing half-way. "Or let another watch."

My body relaxed. So this was what he'd been leading to. The gossips in the organization had said Myre liked to watch. I always thought he liked seeing two Omegas play together. It seemed more taboo, more Myre-like.

"I'm sorry," I said, turning my head to the side.

"Sorry for what?" Myre asked.

"I don't do that. Ever."

"Not even to maybe make an exception?"

"No."

Sam would be furious with me. He'd have told me to go ahead and seduce Myre even more. Win him to me intimately in every way, even that way. I had lines I wouldn't cross. But I kept thinking of Kee, seeing him in those ripped jeans, his naked chest gleaming, his eyes shining. His dancing body in the short black robe when he'd been in the more hyper state of withdrawal.

I felt both protective and oddly proprietary. In truth, though I'd thought about renting chattel for my next Burn, I couldn't stomach the thought of being in the presence of another Omega for sex. I wanted to go home to Kee only, and simply see what he'd been up to. And as for Kee, though I knew eventually I would have no right to control him, just the thought of him with another Alpha made my mind spin, then stop.

This was the first time I'd actually faced, straight on, this non-rational response to having Kee living in my apartment, touching all my things, remaking it to his tastes.

Myre looked at me and while I felt good at a job well done—Sam would be ecstatic—that gaze was toxic.

"You say no. Just like that." Myre sounded anything but pleased.

"I'm sorry, sir. It's just a thing with me."

"I don't believe in the old adage never mix pleasure with business. You know that."

"Yes. And you have treated me very well with fancy dinners and gifts and my salary. And the car." He'd given me so much. "But I have my weird tastes, and my ways."

"So no sharing. Now that we've got that out in the open," Myre said.

I waited for the rest of that sentence. The hammer to drop. The wrath to descend.

I wanted to smooth things over. If it got tense between us, the entire job would be at stake. Not only my place in Myre's organization, but my field work position. I'd been at this two years. If I didn't bring results, it would be considered a failure and I didn't want to think about how that would be addressed regarding me and my future.

'You appeal to me," Myre said boldly. "I want you to know that."

"And I am honored," I replied. "But I am oriented to Omegas only. And when I am in the Burn, very territorial."

"Ah, yes. I should have expected it from you. Your Alpha strength shows through in ways you may not be aware of."

I raised my eyebrows.

"I'm pleased to have you at my side. Please assure me there is no discomfort between us now."

"No, sir. You do honor me." I forced a smile.

"It isn't easy figuring you out. You do not give away tells, as we say. You are careful. Very careful."

I heard menace in those words, but maybe it was my imagination. Myre had literally just thrown himself at me. After telling me he watched me carefully. After asking me such personal questions.

There was discomfort, but my training kicked in and I didn't show it.

I needed to make a report to Sam. I was well overdue. But he was used to that. Now I didn't dare. If Myre watched me even closer now, that put Kee in danger.

My hackles rose. I had some plans up my sleeve. Maybe I could finish this job earlier than anyone, including Sam, ever expected.

Kee needed to remain safe. This man had to go down.

Chapter Thirteen

Kee

Bast came through the front door like an Alpha in the Burn. I heard it before saw it.

I jumped down off the ladder in the bedroom where I'd been struggling with getting the ceiling molding painted just right, and stopped at the threshold, facing the living room where Bast still stood by the door.

Bast's eyes flashed like dark suns, the gravity holding me almost frozen.

"Has anyone been here?"

"What? No *hello*? You've been gone two days, Bast."

"Answer my question!"

"No. No one. And like you told me to do last week, I let the deliveries stay on the porch until the truck drives away."

He turned, glancing at all the windows, at the curtains drawn tight, at the TV which was playing music but not blaring.

"I swear, no one has been here," I repeated. "Why?"

He took a few deep breaths.

"Bast." I started to walk toward him. "Did something happen?"

He shook his head.

"Are we in danger?"

"I'm not. You have always been in danger. I've been trying and trying to make you understand that."

"I do understand."

He slid his long, black jacket off and hung it on the hook by the door. Then he emptied his pockets of his wallet and keys and set them on the front table.

Under his breath, Bast said, "I'd move you out of here if I had somewhere to move you to."

My heart sank. I glanced at the bedroom and its new colors of pale blue, with dark purple as an accent. I'd worked on it for days. Now it sounded like all Bast wanted was to be rid of me. I was a burden. An added weight on his shoulders. My very presence risked his dark job, and his own life.

I hadn't asked him to help me. He'd done it on his own. Was he having regrets?

"I swear I'm careful. I'm so careful. And I've lived on my own for years. I *can* take care of myself." I put my chin up to emphasize that last sentence.

Bast hadn't moved. He was framed by the closed front door. A long silence stretched between us. He was all black edges and dark light tonight, his mouth tight, the muscles under his clothing bulging with tension. Strong. Powerful. The kind of Alpha I loved in bed, more than his size, but exuding confidence, the kind who didn't normally shop the streets for Omegas, but had them lining up, or rented them from expensive farms and cloister houses.

My body gave a little tremor at the thought, one of many I'd had of Bast holding me, covering me, thrusting in and out of me.

It had been two days. I'd worked hard, but I'd been so lonely. Bast couldn't even text me. I'd worried, I'd worked, I'd waited.

And now here he was. It was a given that I'd have a visceral, erotic response to him being near.

Finally, he spoke. "I know you can take care of yourself under normal circumstances. This is anything but normal."

"You don't think I know that?" I held out my hand with the splint. It didn't hurt much anymore, unless I bumped it. My toe looked all black and blue, the cut mostly healed, and did not hurt at all, for which I was grateful.

"Do not take this lightly!" Bast's entire body tensed. His face hardened and his lips opened and for a moment I thought he might growl.

I took a step forward. I didn't feel fear, though maybe I should have, but more of an intense worry. My immediate thought was to reassure him. "Bast. I'm fine. No one has come by here."

"It doesn't mean they aren't watching."

"Did something happen over these past two days?" I took more steps toward him. "Bast, something happened. Tell me."

I was within touching distance now. What would he do if I reached out? Before I could find out, he turned away slightly, not meeting my eyes. His voice came out flat and low.

"Myre said things. To me. He could smell an Omega on me."

I nodded and shivered at the same time. "He knows what I smell like."

"I have been using scent blockers so he can't smell any specific scent from me or you."

"Okay then, it's not that suspicious," I offered. "Alphas see Omegas, some of them very often. It's not unusual." Now I gambled on reaching out and touching his sleeve. He glanced at my hand. I kept it there, pressing in a little.

"No. It isn't. Myre is old. But he still has some interest. He asked if he could watch me."

"Watch you?"

"With an Omega."

My mouth dropped open.

"He's too curious about me," Bast continued. "He has been in the past, but back then I was on the job all the time. Day and night. He already saw everything."

"You're still on the job day and night. You've been gone two days," I said.

"But he wants to know what I'm up to even when I'm gone for a short while. I need you to understand how important it is to be careful."

Now I clasped my fingers around his forearm. "I do understand. So what did you say?"

"Say?" His eyebrows went up.

"About his proposal. Watching you." I realized this was not a funny situation and I needed to be more serious. "I mean, it's kind of creepy coming from that guy, okay?"

"Of course I said no."

"Was he mad or weird?" I had experience with rebuffed Alphas. Some of them were not pretty when their egos were bruised.

"He was unreadable. Flat."

"Ahh, yes. I've seen it a hundred times."

"You have?" Now he seemed interested in my opinion. For once.

"Yes. It may be that he's not angry, but it also means he's not totally okay about the rejection."

Bast blinked at me. I almost heard him ask what to do, but he kept silent.

"He knows you well, yes?" I asked.

Bast nodded.

"He knows you're like this." I squeezed his arm. "Pretty unapproachable to most, I would think." I gave him a soft smile. "And private. You're allowed to be that way. If he thinks it's weird, too bad. He's weird. Very weird. Very cold when he was questioning me, like I was nothing more than shit on his heel. He'd just find out where it came from, clean up the mess, and think no more about it. I was not a person. I was an annoyance." I felt my heart beat harder. "He kept asking me the same questions like he was looking for different answers. He didn't bother to really even look at me."

A darkness seeped into my vision at the memory. I had known that was my last night on Earth. Myre had known. He didn't care. The only one who'd cared was Bast. Bast may have struck me as aloof and closed in, but I'd known he wasn't like the others the moment he'd handed me the glass of soda when I'd been locked up.

"He is an Alpha without a soul," Bast half-whispered.

I blinked away my bad memories. Bast faced me now, his eyes more brown than black and smoothing at the edges, his firm jaw softening, strips of his dark hair hanging to the sides, not so neat after a long day, but so pretty where they reflected almost blue in the living room light.

"Then why in all the hells do you work for him?"

"One day I'll tell you." He kept his voice softer than I'd ever heard it. "But please don't ask me that question right now."

Bast had secrets, of course. Why should I be surprised? I could surmise his reasoning all day. Perhaps he had debts from bad choices in his youth. Perhaps he was simply good at his job and found no better boss to work for. Whatever his reasons, I still trusted him. He had saved me. I could see he wasn't a bad man. It was crystal clear despite his job and his dark demeanor.

"I won't ask, then," I replied. My face was so close to Bast's, I could feel his breath on my nose and cheeks. Warm puffs of air. His tight chest rising and falling in his anxious state.

Was it all for fear of my safety? My heart felt like hot liquid at the thought. "I'm fine. I'm safe, thanks to you."

His eyes closed, then opened again. Staring right into mine. Burnt amber. Deep and dark as newly turned earth. He said, his breath fluttering against my face, "I need to do better. If anything happened to you--"

"Why?" What was I to him? No one. A lowly street boy. An addict. Worthless.

In a matter of about two seconds, between one breath and the next, Bast stepped into the final space between us. His dark head bent. His hands came up as mine fell away, and he grasped me just below the shoulders. Then his lips were on mine, sudden and warm, at the same time unyielding but soft.

128

His mouth on mine, still closed, embraced my whole body, that kiss was so encompassing. Along with his scent of burnt edges and sweetness, his tall body though not touching felt like it brushed up all over me as intense electrical flashes of pleasure zoomed through me from head to toe.

My impulse was to open to him in every way. Mouth, arms, mind, body. Bend and go with it. Offer myself. But this wasn't some quickie for a paycheck. This was Bast, all tight edges and controlled orbits of dark that contained him. Kept him organized and on point and it was how he had managed, with everything going against the result, to somehow make sure I lived despite the orders of a man who seemed to own all the streets in the city. And him.

Bast's lips were hot just as I'd secretly imagined. His grip strong. His demeanor all-encompassing. I breathed him in, all smoke and amber, and held myself very still. My impulses didn't necessarily rule my instincts, and my instinct told me to be patient. Go slow.

But I couldn't help but think: What was this? An Alpha control thing? Or something more?

Something more. I had to believe it. He'd been worried the moment he'd walked through the door tonight. Afraid for more than just his job. Afraid for me.

When Bast pulled back, his eyes were two storms brewing. I wanted to be pulled in. At the same time, I braced myself.

"Don't worry. It's not the Burn."

I nodded, licking my lips and tasting him spice-sweet upon them.

Bast's lower lip trembled as I watched something pass over his face. Then he pushed by me, gently, and headed for the kitchen.

I turned and watched him, still hardly daring to breathe.

Finally, I followed him and stood in the kitchen door while I watched him prepare a sandwich.

"Want one?" he asked without looking up.

I had worked long hours in the bedroom finishing up the paint job. I was starving. "Yes."

He made two turkey sandwiches, garnished them with pickles and lettuce, and cut open a green apple, sliced it, and added it to the side. Without looking at me, he handed me a plate and brushed by me again to go into the living room to his usual spot. There, he turned on the TV and sat.

I took my place on the couch. My body burning.

Slowly, I chewed my sandwich. I could tell it was great. He used lots of mayo and fresh turkey from the deli where he shopped. But honestly, I didn't taste a thing. I chewed methodically, swallowing hard.

I drew my legs up beneath me and continued to eat, not really looking at him, but focusing only on him out of my peripheral vision.

He sat upright and still, the only movement was his jaw as he chewed, and his hand lifting the sandwich to his mouth. I knew he wasn't hungry. He already told me he'd had a strange dinner with Myre. Maybe he hadn't eaten much, but I figured he had prepared the meal to distract himself. To not think about what he'd just done.

Kissing me.

It could have been the silhouette of a ghost sitting in the chair beside the couch. A man not really there. This all could have been a dream.

My cock twitched, telling me it didn't think this was a dream at all. This was real. This Alpha had an effect on me.

I finished my sandwich and apple slices, glancing quickly at Bast's plate as I set my own on the coffee table and grabbed my water.

Bast had barely eaten any of his meal.

I let the TV play some inane sitcom a little longer, then turned to him, folding my legs so my feet were centered at my crotch, and leaned forward.

"May we please talk?"

130

Bast turned to look at me. He swallowed. I saw muscles twitch in his face. His eyes were flashes of obsidian. "No."

I leaned forward a little more, bouncing a little. "Yes." I kept my voice as soft and low as possible.

"All right." He put his plate in his lap. "I'm thinking it might be better if I take you to a hotel. One I know is not associated in any way with Myre."

"Hmm. Yes, I've been airing the bedroom. I opened the windows, but having to keep the curtains shut prohibits the smell of paint from fading. It's a slow process."

"That's not why."

I nodded, clasping my hands. "You don't think I'm safe here anymore."

"No."

"All right." I jumped up. "I can pack very quickly. I have very little. Let's go."

He stared at me. "It will be just you."

"Alone?" My heart fluttered in fear. He couldn't leave me. Not now.

"Yes."

"And about what just happened? When you were standing at the door—"

"We need not discuss it. It was thoughtless on my part. A mistake."

"Didn't feel like a mistake to me." I touched my lips, then took a step toward him. "Not at all."

"It was. I didn't mean for it—" He stopped. He kept interrupting his own thoughts and I knew it was because he still didn't have complete control of them.

"It's all right." I winced at my unfortunate choice of words. I'd meant to say something more along the lines of, "It was great." Something better than all right.

He shook his head. "You need to be safe. The issue cannot be confused with that."

But I wasn't confused. I was clear. He had saved me and I was grateful, but I wasn't okay with the kiss because of that.

Bast interested me beyond his mystery and long dark coat and perfectly combed back hair. He was a bad man, but something didn't track with that, because my heart told me he wasn't. I was intrigued from day one and I missed him when he wasn't around.

I tended to be nosy so I'd gotten bored and gone through everything in the little apartment. Everything he owned. He kept little in the way of possessions, but his computer which was set up in his bedroom and locked, had been easy to override and navigate.

I found he followed a lot of articles and social media on investigations into Myre and his organization. I also discovered he had interests in various things including: baseball, men's fashion, and of all things, Omega rights. That last one threw me. And told me so much about who I was dealing with. Up until that discovery, I had thought he saw me as a non-entity. Not so much now. If he did think I was pathetic, that was another thing altogether.

I'd also discovered his stash of porn. Typical for an Alpha. Alpha on Omega—pretty young Omegas, of course. But he also had watched ones where the Omega called their Alpha Daddy, and assorted other kinks. None of which I had any objection to.

He seemed the type, though, who'd never played any of that out. So withheld and withdrawn. Not someone comfortable inside himself perhaps.

I took another step toward him. "You are keeping me safe. I'm grateful. But that's not why I loved what you did. At the door."

He made no response.

"Kissing me," I prompted.

Now he glanced away. "Get your things, then. We are leaving."'

I let out a loud, frustrated breath. "So do you think you were followed or something?" I wasn't scared. I had come to see Bast as the type who made plans six steps ahead. "You're one of

Myre's most trusted men. And you told me yourself you were being so careful."

"I was not followed. Myre has never been here, but he could probably find this place if he wanted to."

It occurred to me yet again that my presence put Bast in danger. I could have left at any time to face things on my own, but then again, if I were seen, if I were caught, Bast would be in danger as well as it became apparent he did not do his job by following orders to kill me. If I stayed and got caught or if I left and got caught the result would be the same.

With a bag in hand of all the things I'd accumulated while staying in Bast's apartment, we left in cover of night. It was the first time I'd been out in so long—other than the patio area outside the kitchen—that I breathed deep. The air smelled good, like cool night and dew.

Bast hurried me to his car, his arm around my waist. It felt good. I was safe with him—I instinctively knew it.

I looked to see he had brought nothing but his long coat.

"You aren't taking anything?" I asked.

"I told you, I'm not staying."

"You can't just leave me all alone." I said it matter-of-factly, but inside I was disappointed.

Bast drove for a long time. I lost track of the minutes. When we were outside the city, smaller suburbs appeared, smaller cities with their lights further apart and their buildings shorter than downtown, like big shrubs on the horizon.

Somewhere past the valleys and hills that surrounded the city, we came upon another area of activity and industry. I didn't know the name of the sector, but I saw hotels and restaurants, car sale lots and malls. We pulled into the nicest-looking hotel of all, with a drive up valet and a fountain out front.

Bast made me wait until he checked in. When he came back, he quickly got me out, giving his key to the valet, and escorted me into the lobby.

It wasn't too busy and no one paid any attention to us. My heart sank to realize I would be staying here for an unspecified amount of time. It was luxurious but boring. I knew he would not want me to leave the room, not even to exercise or swim or go to the game room. And especially off-limits were the bars.

He whisked me into an elevator. I stood beside him, breathing him in. Wanting him as I had on the drive all the way here. Needing him. My eyes prickling at the edges to know he would leave me and I desired him. I yearned for that kiss again.

I hated being alone. I'd never been alone my whole life. The streets were my friend. All the people who lived there. All the bar and club-hoppers. I'd grown up in that environment. It was always alive, always dramatic and semi-glamorous. I lived with that noise and other people around me day in and day out. The reprieve from that, and getting off the steam, had been different and even good, but I was lonely.

The elevator doors opened onto an ornate hallway with crystal chandeliers and glass tables by the elevator alcove decorated with vases of flowers. The air smelled of pine cleaning fluids and antiseptic wipes. Everything was spic and span.

The carpet was thick against our footsteps. We did not make a sound as we walked. Bast led me halfway down the hall to a door number 733 and opened it with a key card.

The room smelled as clean as the hall when I stepped into the darkness. Behind me, Bast turned on a main light and there was a couch, a table, easy chairs, and a bed. A microwave sat on a counter by the TV. Everything was done up in peach and blue and pale lavender. It was pretty. A comfortable room. A peaceful room for travelers who want to relax, eat well and sleep well.

"It's nice." My voice wavered, soft. I set my small bag on the foot of the bed.

"You will be safe here." Bast spoke as if he had all the facts to that statement figured out in advance, and knew he was speaking a truth and not speculation.

"I can help pay," I began. "I have money stashed in a safe deposit box." It was the only thing a bank allowed an Omega to have without a guardian to co-sign.

"You don't need to," Bast said. "I have it."

I turned to face him. He stood closer to the door than the bed, as if keeping his way clear to flee should he need to. It was amusing, of course. I was sure I neither intimidated nor scared of him. In fact, the reverse was truer.

I took a deep breath. "I—I want you to know how grateful I am."

He looked down and away without moving his head.

I took a step forward. "Bast, I--"

He put his hand up to stop me. I shut up, blinking fast.

"You'll be fine," he repeated. "You can order room service on the room's account. Any movie on TV, anything you want. Just don't leave this room."

I felt like a prince in an ivory tower. It was the whole fairy tale scenario except no dragon guarded me. And the only prince who might come to rescue me was Bast, who looked as if he couldn't wait to leave.

"You have everything you need."

I frowned, trying to nod, but could not complete the gesture. "Not company."

He glanced up. When I met his eyes, he managed to hold my gaze.

"Bast," I near-whispered. "Please don't leave me all alone. At least, not for tonight."

It was a daring statement to this man, this gangster.

He opened his mouth as if to answer but before he could say anything, I took another step forward. "Please!"

I wanted companionship. But more, I wanted him. Bast. The bad man who'd risked everything to save my life. I didn't want to beg, but I would if I had to. My breath hitched.

Chapter Fourteen

Bast

"Please."

Kee's green eyes shimmered.

I'd promised myself I wasn't going to let this happen. To become personally involved with anything pertaining to my job was unprofessional. It could lead to utter disaster. My paranoia over Myre's interest in my life outside the job should have been unwarranted.

But I'd already let myself become personally involved when I'd saved Kee's life. And then I'd kissed him.

That kiss. I still felt it clinging to my lips, warm and lush and sweet. A surprise for me. I didn't think Kee did *sweet*. And that wasn't *my* usual procedure, either.

Kee made me confused. I wasn't in the Burn, so I had no excuses. But I wanted him. Against all my training to remain apart from the job emotionally, I wanted him.

I took a step forward. Willing or unwilling. I couldn't decide.

For two years I'd been living a lie. I'd kept my Omega partners distant and hired temporarily to the parameters of my Burn. When Myre threw lavish parties, I participated only sometimes, and only took Omegas to my bed privately, rarely. And then mostly for appearances. My focus was elsewhere. On the job.

"You kissed me on purpose. It wasn't for nothing." Kee's voice tangled in my mind, low and almost shy, which was completely outside his bubbly personality. He took a deep breath and his injured hand nervously shook.

Something turned over in my chest, the hold there I'd maintained for so long breaking, like ice melting as warmth suffused my body.

I reached out and took his hand gently in mine, holding it still.

He looked up at me with such hope—and something else glimmering in his gaze. Something both hungry and soft, trembling.

I'd never felt such a pull to another human being before. My body responded in a sort of fever not unlike the Burn, but sweeter, less gritty.

I shook my head but it didn't help. I couldn't control this.

"Come here." My other hand shot out and gripped him by the waist, yanking his body toward mine.

I leaned down and put my lips to his and this time the kiss seared me from the inside out until I was surrounded by heat and desire and him. *Kee.*

Kee's own arms came around my shoulders as he pressed his body to mine.

My cock went instantly hard.

Kee was not small, nor short, and as he pushed against me I felt his own hardness beneath his jeans rub against my own and collide with my thigh.

All I wanted to do was pick him up in my arms and lay him on the bed. I wanted to touch him everywhere, learn him, know him. I wanted to arouse his beautiful body and watch him come apart. I wanted to be inside him moving, clinging, knotting, as he held me tight and kissed me and ran his hands up and down my back.

We both opened our mouths at the same time and Kee gave a soft moan. The urge to mate him became overwhelming. No, not mate. Make love. I wanted to make love to him until the world ended. My focus was off, my vision blurred, and I found myself making a sudden turn and grabbing Kee, lifting him off his feet into my arms, cradling him against my chest.

He wasn't heavy—not to my strength. The few steps to make it to the bed were easy and fast as I slung him down upon it, trying to be gentle through my eagerness.

His head fell back, exposing his neck. I saw his chest rise and fall with his deep, aroused breaths. I watched his pink lips part. "Bast! Yes!" The words were made up of a hiss and a moan.

He spread his legs and I knelt between them, leaning over him and burying my face in the crook of his neck, inhaling him, nipping and licking at the side of his throat.

My cock throbbed against my trousers. Needing friction. Wanting attention. It was too fast. Too fast. I wanted to go slow. I wanted to savor him.

I pulled myself onto my side and Kee turned to face me, a gentle smile shivering his mouth. We both gravitated toward each other and kissed again, our arms around each other, and if possible it both cooled and heated me at the same time. At least it gave me a moment to relax into this, not just to shove, pry, take.

I brought my hand up to the back of his head and curled my fingers around a handful of his shining dark hair. It was the texture of satin ribbon, and I weaved my fingers through it to feel more of it.

When we both pulled back for breath, Kee said, "I want you, Bast. I want you so bad."

All words stopped in the back of my throat as if there were a block there. I could only breathe strained and the noise that came out was a yearning groan.

I lost track of how many times we kissed, or how often my mouth strayed from Kee's lips to his jaw, to his throat and the top of his chest. He was wearing his old vest, which I'd laundered along with his torn-up jeans. The material was soft and worn, and did not fasten in front. It exposed his chest and stomach like the street boy he was, but in a way that appeared more elegant than crude. None of that mattered to me, really, for I found him quite lovely in anything he wore, including my short black robe.

But now I wanted skin. I brought my hands forward and pushed at the cloth at his shoulders. He knew instantly what I wanted, and shrugged out of the vest, bumping against me as he did and sending me into even more desire for him.

He lay back, chest naked and gleaming, a half-grin on his face, and his hands went to his jeans, deftly undoing the button and zipper.

Mesmerized, I rose up on one elbow and watched him shimmy out of them. He'd gone commando—no underwear. He expertly kicked off his shoes and drew his legs up, knees bent, to kick the jeans all the way off.

My gaze went up his naked legs and up and up until it settled on his stiff cock, straining hard and flushed against his flat abdomen. He was uncut, as most Omegas were. He was so aroused the naked tip poked out from the loose skin, shiny and a slight paler pink than the smooth shaft.

My mouth watered. He was the prettiest Omega I'd ever seen, and now I saw he had the prettiest cock. Ever. I licked at his ribs, then his stomach.

When I licked over the head of his cock, so plush and full, he cried out. "Bast!"

I wanted it. All of it. I sucked him down all the way, needing to taste him, to feel him throb and need and beg. I wanted him to want me. I needed it.

My own cock spasmed in empathy.

Kee moaned over and over, his head tossing right to left on the bedcover.

I tongued around the base of his cock before pulling up, sucking hard, and then tongue-teasing the tip. Kee groaned louder and half sat up as I continued my teasing of him.

"Don't make me come too fast. Please!"

I took my mouth off him and said, "You want this."

"Yes, but—"

I sucked the tip in again, playing my tongue in circles around it.

"Oh!" he yelled.

I reached between his legs to massage his balls which for an Omega were ample. I liked it. Then my fingers trailed further back to encounter a slickness, and his crack. He was already wet for me.

I sucked only the head of his cock while I explored that area until I found the hole and slipped in a finger.

Kee moaned and said, "Now you're just being unfair."

I took my mouth off him and looked at his face. It was rapt, just the way I'd wanted to see it. As I wiggled my finger, his mouth dropped open and he inhaled sharply. His hard cock leaked as well. He was a total mess.

Finally, he shook himself toward some sort of focus and reached up to me, grabbing at my shirt. "Off," he said.

"You're very demanding."

"Then you command me." He added, with emphasis. *"Daddy."*

That word went straight to my core. How did he know? I wanted to be that for him. Give him everything. Right now. Anything he wanted.

"If you're good," I said.

"I will be."

My body went hotter, if possible. My need was nearly uncontrollable. He was playing right into my most secret fantasies.

I was still wearing all my clothes, including my long coat. I sat up and shrugged it off, then the shirt in record time. I reached for the button on my trousers, but suddenly Kee sat up and grabbed my hands.

"Let me," he said.

I leaned back a little toward the head of the bed and watched Kee's hands, so close to my hard-on, slowly and gracefully undo the button and slip the zipper down. He parted the cloth. I lifted my hips so he could tug it down, along with my briefs.

He had deft fingers, even with the broken one, which he kept aloft and out of the way.

My cock popped free and stuck straight up, thick and long, aching.

"Yes, that's it," Kee said. Nothing more.

He leaned down and gave it a lick. Then teased me with his tongue, possibly in retaliation for what I'd just done to him. I was happy he wanted to even things up. It was amazing, those quick licks, the heat of his mouth against my hot flesh.

My tip spurted pre-cum and Kee licked it away, moistening his lips. Then he sucked me into his mouth so sweetly I thought my entire body would explode. I thought I would come right then. I hadn't done that—come so fast—since I'd been eighteen and in my first Burn.

But I held on. Just barely. Kee seemed to know not to use too much friction or sucking, maintaining me on edge but not falling over it.

As he moved his mouth over me, he nudged my trousers all the way off and I heard them drop to the floor with a shushing sound. Then his hands went up and down my thighs, and he sucked me deeper into his mouth.

My cock spasmed but not to full orgasm, and I felt more pre-cum gush out. He pulled slowly up and off. Then he just stared at me over my jutting hardness, his gaze intense, thirsty, glazed.

He spread his good hand around the base of my cock as he continued to look at me, massaging lightly.

"I want this. In me. Knot and all. Think you can do that?"

I sat up then, tipping him over and onto his back. "Only good boys get the knot."

"Oh." He tilted his head on the pillow. "Well." A smile. "I'm very very good."

Then he lifted his legs and spread them, pulling them back, wrapping his hands around the backs of his thighs. His hips rocked up and in that position his crack was spread, his lovely lush cheeks straining. His hole was wet and dark, pink around the edges, completely devoid of hair. It was ready. It was waiting.

I didn't want to wait. I got between his legs and put my hand there, touching him, feeling how open he was, how malleable, how ready. I easily slid in two fingers and he hissed.

"That's very good," I said.

He gave a heavy sigh. "I know."

When I glanced up at that response, I saw his grin.

My cock gushed again at the thought of being inside him. We were both very wet and very ready. Not all Omegas were easily slickened like this. Some needed extra lube, but with Kee lube would have been redundant. That step could be skipped.

"Do it now," Kee hissed.

I looked down at him, so amazing, so wanton. And all for me. I tried not to think that he was trained for this, that maybe it was just his libido and not me. Any Alpha would do in a pinch. But he seemed to want me. And I told myself it was okay, that I was that Alpha. That I could be the one he could call Daddy if that was what he wanted. Certainly, I wanted it. More than he could know.

"Put that big Daddy cock inside me. I need it. Please."

I grabbed myself and lined up, the tip rubbing at his hole. So good. So slippery. Slippery was good because the friction would be a little less and I would last longer.

I flexed my hips and pushed in. Immediately, Kee's body, though tight, opened to me, and his muscles throbbed against my tip. I pushed a little harder and it popped in. Then his entire channel seemed to suck on me, tugging as I pushed a little more. His body just sucked me in to fire and silken pleasure before I knew what was what.

I found myself speaking before I knew what I was saying. "You're such a good good boy. So good!"

"Thrust," he cried out. "Please!"

"So good. You've been so good. You've earned it," I said.

I pulled out to the tip, then pushed back in. Slow at first, then steadily gaining my pace as I did it a few more times. Kee held himself open and his moans encouraged me.

We were matched for pace as he rocked his body toward mine over and over. We were truly fucking now. There was no going back. It was real and solid and better than anyone I'd ever had.

My cock pistoned in and out of him, alive and so sensitive the chills of pleasure coursed throughout my chest and limbs and brain. I was blurred with desire, but I could still see him before me, laid out all burnished golden skin, his lovely cock pressed hard and tight to his lower stomach. I had been holding onto his hips after I entered him, but now I moved one hand to curl around his erection.

He squirmed at the contact and his internal muscles tightened making me groan aloud. I felt the burning at the base of my cock, and the tension there, as it prepared to form a knot.

I didn't normally knot Omegas unless I was really horny, or really liked them. Not even in my Burns. But this was automatic. I had no control. The knot was forming, wanting to come along for the ride as my whole body responded to Kee.

I would not be able to hold back in a minute. Maybe less.

Kee's head was all the way back, and he moaned again and again. He called my name and suddenly his cock was jolting and jerking in my hand, spraying come into the air and all over his chest.

His anal muscles tightened again, milking me harder and I thrust all the way in and burst inside him with a yell. His entrance clamped down and the muscles went to work on me as my knot began at the base of my cock. The muscles moved against the knot, firm, trapping my cock, and then we were stuck together.

"Oh, yes!" Kee nearly screamed. "Give me that Daddy knot now!"

I tried to thrust deeper but I was all the way in. I leaned over him, my hands now on either side of his chest, and nearly collapsed onto him. He wrapped his legs about my hips and held me in place as I huffed heavily against his neck.

"Oh," he breathed. "That's so wonderful! Oh, thank you, thank you!"

As my knot expanded and started to move, I felt more liquid spurt from the head of my cock inside him in an orgasmic whoosh. I moaned into him, and he hugged me closer.

"Yes, that's it."

His muscles pressed and released over and over. "I'm coming inside, too," he whispered breathlessly.

We lay together in ecstasy, linked, pleasure coursing through us both.

His hands stroked my hair, then my back, just as I'd imagined he might. Just as I'd hoped.

Every time my knot moved, another wave of orgasm hit, and Kee moaned along with me. For about fifteen minutes I held this beautiful man beneath me, loving it, feeling every twinge and muscle spasm in him as if it were my own. I never wanted to let him go.

Even when my knot finally released with one last stupendous orgasmic release, we remained connected. Embraced.

Finally, worrying my weight might be making it hard for him to breathe, I rolled us onto our sides and my cock slipped out, still half-hard.

"Oh, I wanted you to stay inside me," he whispered.

I kissed him to take away any feeling of loss he might have, and he invaded me with his tongue immediately. Our nude bodies slipped against each other, our legs entangling.

Kee's hand trailed to my hip and over my buttock. "Mmm." He groaned into the kiss. When he pulled back, he said, "You're such a catch."

"I was thinking the same about you."

He rested his head against my chest, licking intermittently at my throat. For a while, we both dozed. It had been an exuberant first time between us. I wanted more, but I

144

wanted to let him recover a bit first before I made motions to continue.

After a while, I heard Kee speaking through my dazed state.

"I know you think I'm a street boy and get sex all the time, that I'm gutter trash. But this wasn't normal for me."

I'd moved slightly onto my back and he lay with his head on my shoulder, our naked bodies still entwined.

I lifted my head a little, my arms tightening around him.

"I don't think you're trash. I've never thought that."

"But the way your people treated me. And how disgusted you were with me when you found out I was an addict."

"I wasn't disgusted. I was worried. For you, Kee. For your safety. I thought you might run away because of your addiction and put yourself in more danger. The responsibility for an addict merely doubled my workload."

"I thought about it. Running away, I mean."

"I know."

He chuckled into my skin. "I'm not a good boy."

"You kicked it, though. You stuck with it and didn't cheat."

"I still crave it." He wriggled in my arms.

"But you haven't done anything about it."

"But I wanted to."

"Well, that's to be expected."

He wiggled some more, then lifted his head with a snug smile. "You should probably spank me. Then I'll be distracted and so good for you."

I frowned at him, not with irritation but a question.

He winked.

"You little imp. You broke into my computer, didn't you?"

"Who? Me?"

I pushed him over and started to kiss him again.

I got so hot and hard so fast I was spinning. Then Kee turned in my arms and lifted his hips, rear up. His ass was gleaming and tawny and plush. So pretty. Kee was pretty all over and he knew it.

He spread his legs just enough so that when I sat up I saw his cock was rock hard, pointing toward the head of the bed.

His ass faced me and I got on my knees. "With my hand?" I asked.

I'd only ever fantasized about this. I'd never done it.

"Yes. Make me behave." His tone came out petulant, like a little brat.

I stroked his ass first, feeling the contours, the smoothness of the skin, the fullness. How it stretched as he bent for me, and swayed. I ran my hands up and down his thighs.

Finally, I came down hard on his right cheek with my palm.

Kee jerked forward, then said, "Oh!" It was not a sound of pain.

The sting in my palm, and watching his submission, made my cock throb.

I smacked him again on the left cheek, slightly harder to test it.

He giggled. "Oh yes!"

I did it two more times.

"Tell me to behave."

I leaned over him, my hand going between his legs from behind to clutch his hard cock. In his ear, I said, "Oh, I'll tell you, all right."

Then, I sat back, releasing his cock. I snaked it back under his waist to grab it, and as I held it I gave him a rapid succession of smacks.

He cried out and thrust into my grip.

"You are out of control and you know it," I said firmly.

More smacks, along with more stroking.

146

"You are just a little boy who needs to do some growing up."

I wasn't sure after that what I said, but it was a lot about bad boys and good boys, and he raised his ass higher every time to receive the spankings.

When his ass cheeks were good and red and hot to the touch, I stopped. I stroked gently over the skin, then spread him to see he was slick again. Ready.

My cock was raging to be inside him again.

"Do it." The voice came from the pillows, slightly muffled.

I leaned down and licked him from balls to hole.

"Oh gods!" He nearly screamed.

Only when I was good and done torturing him did I position myself from behind, on my knees, my cock jutting out and dripping.

His hole gaped, so ready. His cheeks were so pretty, all ready and flushed from the spanking.

I rubbed at him with the head of my cock, then inserted the head. I slipped in easily and I thrust hard.

Kee gave a grunt. "Harder!"

I began to fuck him, one hand on his lower back, the other gripping his reddened ass cheek to hold him open to me.

And then we were flying.

Chapter Fifteen

Kee

Bast fucked me three times in the hotel room that first night. We slept together wrapped in each other, too hot but too turned on to care about getting under the covers. Only in the early dawn hour did Bast bring a lightweight sheet up to cover us both.

By all the gods, Bast was good in bed. He was clearly the best fuck I'd ever had, touching me everywhere I wanted to be touched before I could say what I craved. When I wanted friction on my cock, he was there, stroking it. When I wanted it sucked, he seemed to read my mind and sucked it. When I wanted to be fucked hard, he provided the thick long cock to take me to places I'd only ever dreamed where the stars were like white snowflakes and everything was intensely euphoric.

Most Alphas ignored Omega cocks, especially if they were in the Burn. They only focused on the hole. We were the hole. That and no more. But Bast wanted my whole body. He wanted to touch me everywhere, explore, grip, soothe, stroke and suckle every part of me.

Most Omegas were okay with attention on only the hole. We loved the touch. We had sensitive spots inside our channels that brought us to orgasm when stimulated. Our internal orgasms were completely wonderful and satisfying. Still, we had cocks and balls. We were male just like our Alpha counterparts.

In the distant past, when females existed, they didn't have cocks. Our designation as male came from that ancient binary gender thing from a time none of us could imagine. But it was stated as a scientific fact; we had cocks and balls. Despite the extra organs that allowed us to conceive and carry children to term, we were still male. All of us, Alpha and Omega alike.

Why Omegas were treated as lesser citizens was confusing to me, and to many of us. The Alpha dominance factor was part of it. They were aggressive and bigger and stronger. So they won out to rule the world.

Omegas were left in the dust.

In more recent but ancient times, Alphas were so aggressive they fought over Omegas. Often, this happened when both Alphas were in the Burn, so they were even more violent and filled with the need to mate. They would enter an arena to make a claim and fight to the death. If they didn't fight to the death, then the victor would rape the other Alpha to show supreme domination and discredit the other down to the notch of Omega, no better than to bend over for other Alphas. The Omega would go with the victor, with no choice in the matter, to be owned by that Alpha for the rest of their life.

Now, claims were made in office buildings with a signature and an official stamp on a card you might carry in your wallet. And Omegas could dispute a claim if they wanted to, but it was complicated and often expensive, leaving us still no better than the chattel we were seen as.

When we finally both woke late in the morning, Bast rose and took me up into his arms the way he had when I was in withdrawal from steam. He set me down in the shower and insisted on bathing me. I wasn't allowed to touch myself.

He took great care over my entire body, and his hands and the soap aroused me all over again. In best *Daddy* mode, he knelt and took care of even that, sucking me dry so that I was limp all over by the time he quickly washed himself. He then took me out of the stall and dried me with a fluffy towel.

He led me back into the room where we kissed as we waited for our room service breakfast. I saw he was aroused, but when I offered myself, he said, "I don't have the time. I have to go back to work after we eat our--" He glanced at the clock. "Brunch."

It was close to eleven. Definitely brunch time.

While we ate, we discussed the food choices, what tasted good, what were our favorites. I was more interested in Bast than I was in the food.

Finally, I said, "Have you ever done that before?"

He looked up. "Done what?"

"Uh." My face flushed. "Spanked someone. And, well, you're really good at daddy care."

He glanced away. "Uh. No."

"So. You're first time, then. You're very good." I bowed my head. "I loved it."

Now he lifted his gaze to mine. "You have done it?"

I nodded. "For pay. Not because it, um, felt right. But with you." I gave him a sheepish smile. "It felt right."

"You're—okay then." He did not make the statement in the form of a question.

"Yes. I loved it." My whole body heated. As big as I was, I wanted to jump over the table and curl into his lap, kiss him and hold onto him and never let go. Instead, we continued to eat.

For some reason, the room seemed incredibly bright. My every sense felt more attuned to the environment.

When Bast dressed and was ready to leave, I stood before him. "Please come back. Tonight. Please. Even if it's really really late."

He nodded. "I'll make an excuse. I'll say I'm going into my Burn a little early. It's not entirely a lie. You make me feel like it's already here."

I couldn't stop my grin. He had told me he had never thought of me as trash, but his words just now—that he'd be back no matter what—confirmed he wanted me. Me. And no one else.

He looked amazing in his long coat. Now that we'd spent the night together, and I saw him more fully, all the hardness had seemed to melt from him in less than a day. His dark eyes glittered, but with desire for me. He was more handsome than anyone I'd ever known.

In bed, I'd marveled at him. His compact, narrow ass. His flat chest, fully muscled, beneath broad shoulders. The narrowing of his waist, the jut of his magnificent cock beneath which swung a tight but large sac of nice round balls. His belly was flat, the belly button shallow and oval instead of round. He had two sweet dimples above his ass that I loved to stroke when he was inside me. His kisses, gods above, his kisses were the deepest and most sincere connection I'd ever felt.

I went to him, wearing only briefs, and pressed my body against his. I didn't want him to leave and go back to work for that craggy old desert-wrinkled boss of his. I didn't want him to be part of that gang.

"I'm afraid," I whispered into his chest.

"You don't have to be afraid. I'll make sure you're safe."

"I'm not afraid for me." I lightly smacked him in the ribs. "For you, Daddy."

"I'll be fine. But you, you naughty boy. You have to stay in this room where you are safe and not leave. Do you hear?"

I nodded, thrilled at his context of the word *naughty*.

When he opened the door and walked into the hall, I held it open for a few seconds, watching him stride away, his long coat flapping at his calves. I never wanted him to leave my sight.

Just as I was about to close the door, I heard the elevator bell in the alcove where Bast was headed. I'm not sure why, but I stepped forward to keep watching him as he made the turn.

But he never did.

Chapter Sixteen

Bast

I knew I smelled like him. Peaches and cream. That was it. My new favorite dessert. I'd used scent blocker before breakfast, but on my way out of the hotel room, Kee had pressed himself tightly against me.

I had no regrets.

Plus, it wasn't wrong for an Alpha to smell of an Omega. All Myre's crew did, off and on. But if Myre recognized Kee's scent on me, there would be a problem. But Myre was old. He didn't have the same fine-tuned senses as young Alphas on the prowl. He didn't fuck Omegas, he watched them fuck. Or observed Alphas fucking them. Which told me he didn't scent them as well. At least not in the way fertile Alphas in the Burn did.

My plan was to walk into Myre's office with my head held high, giving away no evidence that I'd just had the night of my life. It would be work as usual. And then after, I had to find some way to get to my burner phone and call Sam and update him. Let him know I was fine.

As I walked down the hotel hall, my shoes sinking into the thick carpet, I felt Kee watching me. He should have closed the door immediately behind me. He should have done a lot of things, but Kee was Kee. He would no doubt do as he pleased. If only he wouldn't leave the room.

I'd make sure he was spanked thoroughly tonight. My cock twitched at the mere thought.

Part of my mind waited to hear the door click down the hall so I would know he was behind a locked door. The other part focused ahead. Just as I was about to turn the corner for the elevator, I heard the ding of an arriving car. The doors made a soft sound as they opened.

I came within view of the alcove and stopped in my tracks.

Myre stepped through the open threshold. His small, dark eyes met mine, his head went back and his lips parted.

"Ah," he said. Just that one word. But it held everything he meant and in that moment I knew his mind precisely. His thoughts were clear in his body language and the set of his face.

Last night when we'd had dinner had been a test. I'd failed. Somehow. I wasn't sure how. In the two years I'd worked for the man, I'd never indicated interest that I wanted to have a more personal relationship with him. He indicated trust and affection, and I responded with flat gratitude and ever better job performance. I had thought that was sufficient. He always gave me leeway and listened to my advice. He always gave me compliments and gifts.

Three men in black suits followed Myre out of the elevator. One was Stone. Weapons out, they surrounded me.

Myre opened his mouth to speak and everyone was distracted by a startled, "No!" coming from down the hall.

Bare feet on carpet running. Heavy breaths. Kee, in shorts and nothing else, approached. "Please," he yelled. "It's me you want. Not him!"

He ran up to my side and put himself between me and Myre's cronies.

I shut my eyes and clamped down on a building scream.

Now they would kill us both.

"He only saved me because I seduced him. It's nothing more than that. Bast hasn't betrayed you. It's me. Me. I did everything you said. I spied for the cops. I wrote down information when guys I knew worked for you were high or drunk. I did it. All of it!"

Stone said, "Is this the guy we questioned a couple weeks ago? Is he out of his mind?"

When I opened my eyes, I saw Myre frowning as if this were some minor disturbance, like a buzzing fly or an itch you can't scratch.

"The Omega is lying," I said, pushing Kee behind me.

Stone stepped forward and grabbed Kee, yanking him back.

"I'm not!" Kee said, trying to pull away from Stone. "Let me go, you ape!"

Stone laughed, holding him effortlessly. Kee was not small, but Stone was large, and several inches taller than I.

"Bast, how'd you get this Omega to treat you as if you're his bond mate, for fuck's sake! Let me in on your secret." Stone was always so crude.

Myre took a step forward. He did not spare one glance for Kee. Instead, he held my gaze with furious intensity. He had a small pistol in his hand pointed at my chest.

"I trusted you, Sebastian," he began.

I stood my ground, saying nothing, but my heart raced in fear more for Kee than for myself.

"You were my second. I was going to hand the reins of all of it over to you in a few years. And now in one night you've broken my heart. You were the very best. My right hand. You did everything impeccably. And now this! For a mere Omega! And a street trash Omega at that!"

I wondered how he had found us here. How he knew to even look. I wondered if Sam was onto him. Watching. Sometimes Sam watched and I didn't know it. From afar. Or with more of his own agents undercover in positions of which I had no clue.

Mostly, though, Sam was a paper pusher. He couldn't risk too much surveillance for fear of being caught and wrecking the entire job. Every move Sam made was a risk to me and to the ultimate goal of catching Myre red-handed at something he could be put away for the rest of his miserable life.

154

All these thoughts and more rushed through my mind in a matter of seconds. But foremost was how to keep Kee safe. I decided to play the only hand I had.

"You don't need the Omega. He knows nothing. I can tell you who informed on your cousin and his friend," I said.

Myre's angular eyebrows rose. "Indeed? You're in no position to tell me what you want me to do anymore, Sebastian. You'll both come with me. And you won't make a fuss."

"Kee isn't even dressed. You're going to walk him through the hotel lobby like this?"

"Cade," Myre ordered. "Give him your jacket."

Cade grumbled but shoved his arms out of the sleeves of a hip-length leather jacket and handed it to Stone.

Stone said, "Put this on."

Out the corner of my eye, I saw Kee obey.

I saw all the weapons, making a note of how many and what makes and models. Myre's guys were trained to fight. I had assessed them all over time. But there were security cameras everywhere in the hotel and they wouldn't want to risk being seen killing anyone here. Weapons were legal. Murder was not. If we went with them, we'd be away from any prying eyes and we'd never return. I needed to stall them. I needed them to make this scene right here, right now.

"I won't be going anywhere with you, Myre. Unless you release Kee." My tactics. Stall. Tease him with information only I had. If I had to, I'd do anything to ensure Kee's safety.

Myre let out a hard sigh. "Now see reason. I can't let him go. You are not a stupid man. You understand he knows far too much about me, my casino and hotel, my cage room, my men. What do you care anyway? You fucked him and it's sudden love? No, I don't think so, Sebastian. That's not how you operate. Besides, he's supposed to be dead. So you lied to me about killing him. Nobody lies to me."

My face flushed beyond my control. But I held his gaze. "You don't know anything about me."

"The stupid Omega was ready to give himself up for Bast," Stone said. The laugh that followed was loud.

"Shut up," Myre said to Stone without looking away from me. Then to me, "Come with us now or I will shoot the Omega."

I knew he wouldn't do it here. Unless he had someone working here who'd give him access to the camera footage. That little idea made my heart pound. I knew he had no connections to this hotel, but he could pay any amount for anything he wanted.

It was still better odds for me to stand the ground here. "You don't have to shoot him. We can go to my room. We can talk this over."

"It's too late. You know that."

"It isn't. We can work this out."

"You betrayed me."

"I didn't betray you by saving a street Omega for my own devices," I argued.

"You could have asked me for him. I would have given him to you," Myre said. "But you hid him. All this time. What else have you been lying to me about?"

"Nothing. You do not need to risk a scene here. We can talk. In my room."

For a second, I thought Myre hesitated. I was wrong. From one breath to the next, he swung away from me and I heard the pop of his pistol at the same time I heard all four elevator doors ding at once and open.

I spun fast as men in black uniforms streamed out of the elevators and into the alcove. But I didn't focus on them. Everything went into slow motion for me. All sound stopped. My vision narrowed on Kee as he looked at me, eyes wide, mouth opening, lips forming my name. His was the only sound I heard as he said, "That fucking ancient mobster shot me."

I didn't think about the weapons all around, Myre or his men, or the cops surrounding us, obviously shouting orders. All I knew was I was at Kee's side in a split-second, my arms around him, my weight holding him as his body tried to slide to the floor.

I knelt to take him gently into my lap, his head cradled against my chest, the leather jacket crinkling. I could see most of his body as the jacket sides fell back. Chest. Stomach. Abdomen. Thighs and legs. There was no hole, no blood.

I pushed the jacket gently away from his shoulders and then I saw the wound. On his right shoulder just under the clavicle. Small. Red. The blood oozing slowly.

Not fatal.

Thank all the gods that ever were.

I pressed my hand to the wound to staunch the flow of blood. Kee's mouth opened in a grimace this time, but his good arm clasp tightly under my own shoulder, gripping my jacket.

Sound started to return. Vaguely, I heard men giving orders. I heard handcuffs jingling and rights being stated. One of the voices was familiar.

Sam. A hand touched my shoulder. "Bast."

I saw Kee's face go even paler than before.

"Am I hurting you?" I asked him.

"I must be dead," Kee said, voice shaking. "I thought I heard that cop say your name."

"You sure do make it difficult, Bast," Sam said. "I wasn't sure I could wrangle everyone together in time when I saw Myre coming into the hotel."

"You were watching," I said, not looking away from Kee, holding him closer.

"Yes."

Kee's eyebrows went up, then down. "You're an informant?"

I shook my head. "We need to get him to the hospital right way."

"The paramedics are on the way," Sam said. He patted my shoulder.

"No? Not an informant?" Kee asked. "You're lying. Wait. You're a cop. You're a cop? No. That can't be right. Forget I asked. Just forget." His eyelids fluttered. "I think I'm going to pass out," he mumbled.

"You're going to be fine, sweetheart."

He smiled. "Sweetheart. Yeah." His eyes closed.

Chapter Seventeen

Kee

I woke in bed. The sheets were all stiff and not soft like Bast's bed. Or the hotel bed. Not comfortable at all. And the smells were crisp, sharp and antiseptic.

One scent permeated them all. Dark amber incense. A distant campfire. A strong hand had hold of my own.

I opened my eyes and saw the hospital room at a single glance. No, it hadn't been a nightmare after all. I'd been shot.

As I tried to move my arm, I felt the gauze and bandage, thick and wrong. A low ache throbbed in my shoulder.

I squeezed Bast's hand and turned my head to see him.

He had had his eyes closed. Dozing. Quickly, they opened. "Kee?"

I nodded. I couldn't believe I was still alive. And Bast was right here next to me, holding my head in his lap. Bast the cop. Bast my rescuer and hero. I knew I was completely safe. "Well, that was fun. When can I go home?"

"I'm sorry. I'm so sorry," Bast began.

"What are you apologizing for?" I asked. "That I got shot? Or that you never told me you were a cop?"

He looked alarmed. "I couldn't."

We stared at each other for a long time.

"I'm glad you're okay."

"I guess it takes a lot more effort than Myre had to kill me," I replied.

"How are you feeling?"

"Like I just got shot." Then I smiled.

"It's nothing to joke about."

"Yeah. Well." My thoughts turned more serious. "I just want to go home."

Bast winced. "Home? Yes. Uh. Where is that?"

I pouted, then glared. "Well, I was doing a really good paint job, you know. And it still needs finishing touches."

Bast blinked.

"If you'll have me. I mean, try it out for a while?"

Bast bit hard on his lower lip. So hard I thought there might be blood. Then his eyes flashed with sudden excess moisture. He smiled hard, like the way a person does when they're trying to hold back a ton of emotions.

"Yes. Yes! Of course! Try it out for a while."

"Okay, then." I moved to try and sit up. "Let's call that doctor and see about getting me out of here."

Bast said, "Maybe just rest for a little while?"

"No way. I hate hospitals."

Bast helped me sit up. And then I was exhausted. "Well," I said. "Maybe I could leave after another nap."

*

The hospital kept me for a whole day. The bullet had been through and through and had not hit anything vital. I was broken, but not horribly so. The doctors and nurses released me into Bast's tender care.

When we got to his apartment, all my stuff had been delivered from the hotel.

"Did the cops do that?" I asked as Bast got me settled into the—our—bed.

"I asked Sam for a favor."

"I think saving your ass was the favor."

"Yes." He tucked the covers around me.'

"Hey." I pulled them away from my side. "You're not leaving me. Get into bed with me."

He smiled down at me. It was weird, seeing him smile so much. When I'd first met him, I thought him incapable of such an expression.

"First, I'm going to get you juice and water. And your meds by the bed. I'll be right back."

I lay back on the soft pillows, alone in the room, studying the ceiling and the trim around it which I'd painted dark purple. I'd done a great job. The walls of the room itself were a paler blue which offset the dark furniture and the long black curtains and the black bedspread. Most of the new paint smell had faded due to the windows being left open overnight.

It all looked quite pleasant. I was happy with the results but I still needed to do the bathroom door, and the trim around it.

I heard footfalls as Bast entered the room carrying a tray. He'd brought my juice, and he'd made us turkey sandwiches.

"Are we eating in bed?" I asked.

"Yes." He set the tray by my side.

"Oh, decadent!"

He touched my face, cupping my cheek. "I don't think I've thanked you."

"What?"

His dark eyes lowered. "For what you did. Everything."

I frowned. "You saved me."

"No. You disobeyed. You were naughty. But you bought me time. And you offered yourself without thought for my life. I—I could never have asked."

"Huh. Well. Usually I'm thinking only for myself. What I want. I think this time I was pretty selfish, too. I'm irredeemable. I didn't want to live in a world without you."

"Irredeemable, eh?"

"Yeah. It's a fault of mine." I picked up a glass of orange juice and took a sip. "Mmm. Good. Anyway, this fault of mine, it's going to require a lot of discipline, I think."

"You think?" Now his eyes sparkled.

I nodded. "But first dinner. I'm starved. And then maybe a nap?"

"Sounds like a good plan."

"You'll stay with me?"

"I won't leave you."

Later, the lights out, Bast held me gently, making sure my injured shoulder stayed well cushioned. He said, "I almost lost you. I couldn't bear the thought."

I yawned. "Not going anywhere. I promise."

"Good."

"Plus, I have a cop looking out for me now. I couldn't be safer."

His arms tightened about me. I wanted more, but not tonight. Too fucking tired.

But after I healed, I had the plan to seduce this man every which way. From Daddy to boy to his in any way he'd have me.

This had never happened to me before. Wanting a single Alpha and no other. Wanting monogamy. The closest I'd ever come was Tarin. But Tarin, though respectful and nice and rich, didn't entice me the way Bast did. Something about Bast had me from the moment he'd given me the soda in the cage. I had thought he was all in on kidnapping me, that he was a bad boy to the core, but still something about him woke me up inside and set the blood flowing in my veins. He'd created feelings in me that had been dormant for far too long.

We were giving this cohabitation thing a try. But I had a feeling we wouldn't be *trying* for long. We'd simply be there for each other. Always.

When I fell asleep against Bast's chest, I dreamed of the Trenches but they were faded, as if vanishing in a storm of fog and rain. I dreamed all the steam I ever took became a negative space in my body, and that space was filled with Bast's thoughts, his truth. His love. I dreamed we had a bond like a ribbon linking us together and when Bast laughed, I laughed, and when Bast hurt, I hurt. When Bast Burned, I Burned as well.

When I woke, the blue room had become not a guest room for me any longer, but ours. A haven. A realm dedicated to our desire for each other. Our need. Our slow-fast tipping, then falling, into love.

*

A week later, as Bast began to feel his Burn, and I eagerly prepared myself to be there for him for the duration, I remembered I'd not been taking my contraceptive since my kidnapping. My skin had become sensitive and more flushed of late.

Now I knew why.

Bast had knotted me so many times I'd lost count. He couldn't hold back more often than not.

This news was unexpected. Our bond was still so new. I decided to wait to tell him until after his Burn.

Chapter Eighteen

Bast

Kee was all I could focus on day and night. My body was insatiable. My mind craved him like I'd never craved another in my entire life. He wanted me in return in equal measure, always ready for anything, always willing. My Omega street boy. My sweet naughty son who danced on couches to loud music, who made friends everywhere he went, who did as he pleased.

I took my long overdue vacation time from my real job at Investigations. Many things were taken from me that I'd lived with for two years. My bank account where my checks from Myre were deposited was frozen. But some things in my name I did get to keep, much to my surprise. My gold watch. What did the cops need with that? And my car, a gift from Myre, for which I'd been paying insurance and upkeep. I was grateful. I had another car in storage, a black Cobra Mustang, but it was old and had several mechanical problems.

My hidden account with my agent's salary was freed up, and I had accumulated quite a bit there, so I was fine if I wanted to take more time off after my vacation time ended.

Myre had been brought up on charges. His trial was months away, if not longer, but the judge gave him no bail. So he was gone for some time now, and the case against him built stronger every day.

A week after Kee was shot, I woke a bit hot and agitated. Kee slept tightly pressed to my side, palm flat on my ribs, warm and possessive.

Through the bond that was forming between us, like a blue satin ribbon rippling with our growing closeness, we could feel each other's moods: fears, ecstasies, pains, and contentment.

He gave a little moan and wiggled, pressing his naked body closer to mine.

Kee had healed quickly from his wounds. The day his bandages came off, his splint on his finger was removed as well. We spent our days, when Kee was up to it, doing whatever activity sounded fun: parks, the gym, shopping, restaurants, and more. Though Kee loved to dance, we stayed away from clubs, and anything that might tempt him back to his old life.

I checked and re-checked my calendar, and my Burn cycles. Rarely did my Burn manifest early. My cycles were as regular as the sun rising and setting.

But the itch was coming on. I could feel it. There could be no mistake. Three days early.

With our newly forming bond, sharing a Burn meant Kee would become fully bonded to me. I would not be able to hold back. But so far, in our relationship, the term *bond mate* had not been mentioned. We were close enough we didn't really care. It would take care of itself, I figured. When the time came, it would happen unless one of us made a protest to the other.

But in fairness, I wanted the discussion. Kee deserved it. He needed to know he still had choices. I was firm with him in bed, and dominant, but not entirely. He let me know what he wanted. He had a lot of fortitude I'd not seen before in many Omegas.

"I can feel you thinking real hard," Kee murmured against my chest.

"You can?"

"Yes. It's the Burn, right?"

I kissed the wisps of hair at the top of his head. Then leaned and whispered into his ear. "Sweet boy. Yes."

His head moved a little. "Are you early?"

"Yes."

"It's because of what's between us. I can feel it like a pleasant tug, and a need like light so bright it blinds. It wants completion."

We were talking of the bond without using the word.

"What are your thoughts on that?" I asked softly.

"I've never felt this way before. Like I'm floating inside you and I never want to leave."

"But you do have that choice still. You are free again, Kee. Healed and whole. In a position to make all your own decisions again. Even the bad ones. I want you, but I won't use our relationship and my personal discipline of you to hold you back if you need your freedom."

Now he lifted his head. His green eyes met mine. "This is freedom. Like I've never felt. I feel like I can do anything. And that means being with you. I feel like I'm flying but grounded at the same time, and it's comforting knowing I'm not hurting myself anymore. Is that all right?"

"It's better than all right, my sweet. So much better." My desire for him was so strong. I clamped down on my lower lip to try to contain it.

"Don't hide from me." Kee sat up, his hands trailing absently over my chest. His erect cock poked my hip. My own pointed toward my belly button. "Your feelings—they're mine, too. I know what you want."

I blinked at him as he lifted his leg and slowly straddled my hips, his balls settling at the base of my cock, his own erection bouncing a bit against mine. For once in my life, I wasn't strong. I couldn't say it. The words. *Bond. Mate.* It was too much, like opening myself up to extreme risk of mental agony on the off chance Kee, my wild untamed Omega, would say he wanted to wait to fully finalize our bond. Or that he might never be ready.

Blue satin ribbon. A blinding light, as Kee described it. I knew he wanted it. But I was afraid to say the actual words.

"It's okay," Kee said. "I'm a risk. I know. Not your normal Omega. Uneducated. A bit undomesticated, shall we say? Perhaps not the best catch, but—"

I reached up and touched him on the mouth, closing his lips with my fingers. "No more of that. You are perfect. Haven't I told you that just about every day lately?"

166

He shrugged. "Maybe more than once a day."

"Maybe more than twice," I amended, voice low.

He leaned into me. I could feel his breath on my face now, that Omega sweet peaches and cream. "Does that mean maybe you want more?" he asked. "To make this bond I feel between us whole and final? Do you want a real bond mate, Bast?"

My mind swirled at such a question. The beauty of his voice, his body, his words. I pulled him down to me and kissed the lovely mouth. When I pulled back, I said, "Oh yes, my sweet good boy. Oh yes."

"Then take me into your Burn, my love, and knot me and bond me and make me yours forever."

Such words I never thought to hear from any Omega. Not like this. Not with an agenda, but from a pure space of selfless emotional love. I'd never formed an actual relationship before, and now that I knew what it felt like, I wanted nothing more than Kee with me until the end of my days.

"Yes, Kee. Be my bond mate and stay with me always."

"It would be my honor and my joy, with all my heart," he replied, smiling and kissing me at the same time.

Something turned over inside me, like a huge weight shifting, lifting away and leaving only the glow of Kee in its place. At that moment, the Burn kicked in fully, a sensation I'd never had before. I was the sort of Alpha whose Burns were gradual and short. But with Kee, all rules had changed.

"I can feel it," Kee said softly. "Hot and greedy and aching. And oh so good. I'd love a spanking, but that will have to wait. I want you to take me. I want it any way you want it. Fast, slow, hard, soft. I don't care. I just want *you*."

My cock rose up from my belly.

From morning to night, I had Kee in every position I could manage. I devoured him with my mouth, my hands, my rampant cock. The possessiveness of the Burn had never been so strong for me, but then I'd never had any emotional attachment to my partners in the past.

We took breaks only for water and quick bites to eat.

I knotted him every time I fucked him. Every single time. He was irresistible. And he wanted it.

When my senses weren't too addled, I cared for him as often as I was able. I took him into the shower and held him as I bathed him. I made sure he wasn't chafed or hurting in any manner. I was conscious of mood and tone in voice and mind, never once feeling separate from him, always in tune.

It made the Burn less stressful to be with someone I was already in the process of bonding to. Our bond flowered until we moved in unison in bed, like a choreographed dance but unpracticed, unplanned.

Kee giggled when I kept checking his hole to make sure he was fine. He loved the attention. He presented himself to me willingly, brazenly. If I saw he was the least bit too pink there, I would lick him until he yelled for me to breach him. And when I did, I'd put my hand around his waist and stroke him, knowing through our bond he was on the edge. Within seconds, he'd spurt onto the towels I'd laid across the sheets, as his ass sucked me in to utter rapture.

"Bast," he said breathlessly. "Your cock is the perfect fit for me. You should have no worries. I was made for this."

My cock strained to be inside him again and again. His libido matched mine, full force. I never wanted this pleasure to end.

*

The following day, when my Burn began to subside and we rested, still not quite fully sated—would we ever be?—in each other's arms, Kee began kissing the side of my face and my jaw where my rough beard had started to grow in. He stroked my forehead and hair. He kept touching me, pushing his strong, slippery body against mine.

"Are you coherent again?" he asked.

I smacked him lightly on the left buttock.

168

He laughed. "Because I need you to hear me."

"Hear you? Why? I can feel you in the bond. I can sense your happiness and my own entwined, beyond words."

"Yes, but I have one more thing to say. In words. And I want you to hear it with full faculties. Can you do that?"

I opened my eyes as he continued to stroke my face. We were both exhausted, but yes, I could still hear him. "Of course."

"All right. So, here it goes."

I frowned. "This is serious?"

He scrunched his face at me. "Yes. It's about timing."

"What?"

"Timing. You now. When you first kidnapped me. I—I was on pills."

"I know. The steam."

"No, not that." He paused. "Bast, you're pretty smart. Think. Contraceptives pills?"

Now I was fully wide awake and aware. "Oh. Of course. I never thought to ask you because I never thought we'd—"

"We'd get together. I know. You resisted my wiles a lot longer than most Alphas." He chuckled.

"So you're saying this time over the past two days could result in pregnancy. I see."

"No."

"No?" He raised his head. "I—I don't understand."

"Not could result. Did result. I was pregnant before your Burn. I found out just before and then, well, we got busy. But now I'm telling you."

I sat up, dislodging Kee from my chest. "What are you saying?"

"I just said it. Geez!"

"You're pregnant?" My breath hitched. "Kee? You're pregnant with my child?"

He nodded, looking a little scared. "I am. I know it's soon. I know it's abrupt. But I didn't have any way of getting more pills without bringing attention to myself, which you forbade. So it just happened. And it's sudden. And it's a lot. And, and, and--"

"Kee, my sweet Kee." I grabbed him then, and pulled his face to mine for a kiss. My hands held his head tight, my fingers tugging at his hair. "My child," I said, as I gasped for air. "You're carrying my child? Kee, my beautiful beautiful boy."

"Okay," he sighed. A smile grew on his face. "So you're okay with it."

I squeezed his head tighter in my grip, my hands moving slowly down to cup his cheeks. "I love you. Yes, I'm okay with it. Yes!"

Kee reached up between us and touched my face in return. Rubbing at my cheeks and the side of my nose. His hands slipped against my skin.

"Oh. Bast. Don't cry."

"I'm not." I didn't cry. I never cried. I glowered at him, but suddenly could feel it. The water seeping from my eyes. Tears of utter and insane love I couldn't control.

Our final session as the Burn subsided was a long bout of lovemaking. Touching everywhere with reverence instead of abandon, pulling him to me and on my cock as if he were the most precious thing I'd ever touched.

We moved together in synchrony. Our hands went everywhere. He even touched my own hole, something Omegas rarely did unless asked.

Afterward, we lay sated and panting in each other's arms.

"You're perfection," Kee whispered, pressing his forehead to my shoulder.

"You're my whole world now," I replied.

170

Epilogue

Kee

The couch in the living room didn't really need pillows. I had Bast to lean against. Bast to cushion me. I was always sitting on him or leaning against him.

Teasing, he said, "Upholster me and I can be your permanent furniture."

"I don't need to do that. You already have cushioning." I traced over his bulging muscles.

Leaning more heavily against him, I brought my phone up to begin going through weeks of messages.

When I re-installed my phone account to the new device Bast bought me, there were so many texts and messages I was overwhelmed.

A series of over two dozen stood out, however. All from Tarin, the Alpha who'd tried to help me so many times during which I'd seen him through several Burns. He had told me I was his favorite. Shyly, he'd once suggested a bond.

I hadn't been ready to hear from him or anyone. My life was a mess when I knew Tarin. He deserved so much better.

"Ah, Tarin," I said aloud.

Bast turned his head toward me. "The Alpha who'd previously tried to help you?"

I nodded. "Don't be jealous or anything. You're the only one for me. But I really do need to contact him. It's only fair to him. By now he probably thinks I'm dead."

"All right. You don't need my permission."

"Well." I looked up at him, giving him my cute face. "I sort of want it. *Daddy.* He is, after all, a big handsome Alpha."

"Is he, now?"

I nodded.

"Should I be jealous?"

I shrugged, playing him along.

He gave me a bit of a tough look, and said, "But it's my child you're carrying. And me right here." He tapped the side of my head.

"So you won't be mad when I tell you I'm thinking I need to see him? It would be easier all the way around. To reassure him I'm fine. It would only be this one last time, and then I'll never see him again."

"Hmm." The muscles around Bast's shining, dark eyes tightened. "Mad? No. Jealous? Well, you're mine and you know it." He stared at me for a moment. "Do you want me to be jealous?"

I drew my lower lip into my mouth. "Well. Maybe just a little."

"All right then. I'm jealous. Get this done. And get it done quickly. Then come right home and present yourself to me. For discipline."

"Yes, sir, Daddy, sir!" I jumped up. "Can I borrow your car?"

Bast rolled his eyes.

*

The meeting with Tarin went far better than I could ever have imagined. He was ecstatic to see me healthy and alive. And to hear my story, which I only told him enough of to satisfy him.

The best thing for me was to see that in the time I'd been gone, Tarin had found the perfect bond mate for himself. I had worried he would be a bit broken-hearted over me—he'd done so much for me over the past couple years—but instead I saw he had his own Omega now, Alli, and he was very much in love with him.

It made everything easier on both of us. My conscience was cleared as I drove home to Bast, my love, my mate.

172

Frequent spankings. Lovemaking every night. I couldn't have been happier.

A few months later, Bast and I welcomed our new child into the world. A little Alpha who looked just like him, and glowered more than he wailed. We named him Baski, a combination of both our names. And when Bast held him and kissed his downy head for the first time, I nearly cried.

The birth took a few painful hours. Bast was by my side the entire time, telling me I was brave. Brave? No Alpha had ever said that to me. I'd been called many things: arrogant, aggressive, slut, hole, but never that.

In a few months, our apartment became too small for our little family, so we moved to a house far from the city and Bast's old job with Myre, far from the Trenches.

Bast went back to work in more of an investigative role, retiring from field work and undercover assignments.

I found I had an aptitude for art. Specifically, painting. Little Baski would sit and watch me struggle with learning how to paint leaves and flowers and little toy bears for our precious baby boy to hang in his room. Baski himself had a talent for finger painting that rivaled all others in his age group.

Our world had changed. Bast's and mine. My hard-luck life had worn away to reveal in me a worthy Omega, a man who deserved love and a good life.

And Bast, my lover, my bond mate, my Daddy, the man I'd thought was so dark and bad, continued to wear his long, flapping coat and savor me with his dark, flat looks that made my mind soar and my cock hard. He tended to me patiently. He loved me more than his own life.

Bast. The bad Alpha who'd locked me away but given me a soda when I was most defeated. But he wasn't bad. He'd rescued me and brought me back to life in more ways than I could count. He'd always been good. Always. And that would never change.

THE END

Dear Reader:

Thank you for reading *Omega Untamed: The Omega Misfits Book 6.*

I hope you enjoyed Kee's story as much as I did writing it!

Next on my agenda is: 2 Omega Misfits novellas. One will be a Christmas novella. They will both be part of a multi-author giveaway, one in Oct. 2020, and one in Jan. 2021. To keep well-informed about these giveaways, please join my Facebook group or sign up for my newsletter (or both).

Newsletter: http://eepurl.com/cqDVcX

My Facebook group Wendyland. https://www.facebook.com/groups/718074255203918/

In addition to the novellas, I have another stand alone Christmas story in the works, and a new shifter omegaverse series, **Endangered Alphas**, which will premiere starting in 2021! There will also be more intermittent additions to **The Omega Misfits.**

I hope you continue to stay with me on this journey where I continue my discovery of this wonderful omegaverse genre with many more books to come!

About Wendy Rathbone

Read Wendy Rathbone… where imposters and outcasts, princes and lost boys always find their happily every after.

I have written in all genres: sci-fi, fantasy, horror, paranormal, contemporary, erotica, romance. But I keep coming back to romance as the main focus. Gay romance. Male/male romance. The idea of two men falling in love is irresistible to me. It's all I write now.

All my books are available on Amazon and most are in Kindle Unlimited. So if you have the urge, go take a look. See what's on the shelf.

Male/male romance books by Wendy:

The Kingdom of Slaves Series (contemporary fantasy mm romance)

The Slave Palace
The Slave Harem
Master of Halloween (short story)

The Omega Misfits (Omegaverse mm romance)

Trust No Alpha
The Alpha's Fake Mate
Alpha's Embrace
Single Omega Dad
Omega Chattel
Omega Untamed (coming Sept. 15)

The Imposter Series (fantasy mm romance)

The Imposter Prince
The Imposter King

The Moonling Prince Series (fantasy, sci fi mm romance)

The Moonling Prince
The Coming of the Light

The Foundling Series (contemporary billionaire mm romance trilogy)

Rescue Me
Sacrifice Me
Remember Me

The Fantastic Immortals Series (fantasy/myth mm romance)

Ganymede: Abducted by the Gods
Zeus: Conquering his Heart

Stand Alone Novels

Sci Fi MM Romance

Solstice Gift (holiday)
Not Another Hero
Cocky Virgin Prince
Prey
Scoundrel
The Android and the Thief (Second edition coming May 2020)
Letters to an Android

Fantasy MM Romance

Lord Vampyre
Lace
Snow of the White Hills (mm fairy tale)
The Elves of Christmas (holiday fantasy mm romance)

Contemporary MM Romance

Romantically Incorrect
Snowfall and Romance (Christmas novel)
The Bodyguard's Valentine
Buying You

Contact links for Wendy Rathbone:

Come join my newsletter! http://eepurl.com/cqDVcX

Join my Facebook group Wendyland. I post updates, cover reveals, snippets, sales and other fun stuff every day: https://www.facebook.com/groups/718074255203918/

Friend me on Facebook:
https://www.facebook.com/wendy.rathbone.3

Follow my Amazon author page:
https://www.amazon.com/Wendy-Rathbone/e/B00B0O9BMS/ref=dp_byline_cont_ebooks_1

Follow me on Bookbub:
https://www.bookbub.com/authors/wendy-rathbone

TRUST NO ALPHA
The Omega Misfits, Book 1
Wendy Rathbone

It's a world gone mad. The Alphas are out of control. When you discover you're not who you thought you were, the nightmare begins.

KRIS

At age eighteen, life as he knows it is over for Kris. A secret to his nature he was not aware of has been revealed.

Now, kept as a prisoner in a locked room in the mansion of his wealthy father, Kris is at the mercy of Alpha laws and Alpha domination.

Things take a turn for the worse when his own litter mate threatens him, and his father starts behaving strangely around him.

Escape is his only hope. But where can he go in a world that allows him no rights?

THORNE

Marked as a dangerous Alpha, and living a secluded life alone and unloved, Thorne still grieves for the mate whose death he feels responsible for.

Years have passed, and he refuses to even try to function in normal society.

One day he discovers a young man on his property, disheveled, desperate, and scared. He acts like a runaway Omega, but he doesn't smell like one.

What is this boy? And why does Thorne feel an immediate need to protect him? To bond him? To make him his?

A non-shifter, Omegaverse love story of rescue, first time, fertility issues and an HEA. Standalone read. 65,500 words. (While Omegas are birth-fathers in this universe, there is no on-page mpreg in this book.)

THE ALPHA'S FAKE MATE
The Omega Misfits, Book 2
Wendy Rathbone

The Alphas think they own everything. Including people. Well, I'm here to say they don't own me, and I will never let one of those bastards touch me again.

The frenzy of their Burn cannot be trusted. I know from experience. My first time with an Alpha nearly ended in my death. And because of the laws which favor Alpha rights, and place a large number of unbonded, adult Omegas on chattel farms, my abuser can never be tried for his crimes against me.

Omegas are being hurt. Omegas are dying.

All Alphas are violent. Or so I believe. Until I meet Orion.

Ori is everything a guy could want in a mate. Six foot three. Beautiful brown wavy hair. Bright, dark eyes. Muscles like chiseled marble. He even says "please" and "thank you" at all the right times. He's got it all, except he's an Alpha.

Though he has given me a room in his home free of charge, and has signed fake paperwork saying we are bonded so I don't have to answer my attacker's claim, can I trust him?

But now I'm in danger. If I don't take a real mate, my life as I know it will be over. Can I believe in the goodness of Ori? Can I learn to love again?

A non-shifter, fake mate, Alpha/Omega love story. Rescue. First time. Omegaverse. Mpreg. Healing from sexual trauma. (All books in The Omega Misfits series are standalone reads and can be read in any order.) 61k words.

180

ALPHA'S EMBRACE
The Omega Misfits Book 3
Wendy Rathbone

I am Misha. My name was given to me at birth by the doctor who delivered me. I have never known my parents. I live in a ten by ten space with one window, a sink and toilet, a bed and a locked door. Once a day I'm taken to an outdoor exercise area. I am allowed a limited access tablet and tutored online by computer programs. I have one friend I talk to through a tiny crack in the wall. His name is Cedric and he has trouble keeping himself quiet. When he isn't talking to me about monsters and demons, he screams all the time.

Why is my life so isolated and depressing? Because I am a Sylph. Sylphs are the byproduct of illegal Omega to Omega matings. We are all beautiful, but 99.9% are born insane. The rarest of Sylphs, like me, show no outward signs of madness or brain damage, but we live in institutions because we cannot be trusted.

All of us Sylphs who have lived long enough to pass through puberty have hypersexual disorder which makes life even more difficult for us. It is like something Alphas call the Burn, a mating urge Alphas experience once every couple of months.

But we're Sylphs, not Alphas, and this Burn thing? We experience it all the time. It's a huge problem and why we are kept isolated. Most of us don't survive through our teens because of it.

One day, a handsome Alpha comes to interview and study me. He calls himself the Chief of Staff but his real name is Geo. Like magic, I fall in love with him instantly. I do everything I can to seduce him. He will have none of it because touch between an Alpha and a Sylph is taboo. But I have plans. No matter what, I intend to bond him and make him mine. Forever.

A non-shifter Alpha/Omega-Sylph love story of forbidden love, rescue, and HEA. Standalone read. No Mpreg. 58k words

SINGLE OMEGA DAD
The Omega Misfits Book 4
Wendy Rathbone

My new financial guardian, Mathias, is a cold, self-centered, rude-ass Alpha and the son of one of the wealthiest men in the country. To him, I am a burden on society, only fit to live on a chattel farm.

It doesn't matter that I'm drawn to him, to his ominous presence and chiseled jaw, his muscular body in his fitted silk suits. I'm a single dad with kids and responsibilities --I don't have time for that rich bastard.

He keeps coming by the house so I can sign documents, fine. But then he's got cute gifts for my kids.

It's got to stop. I don't have time to fix him. Don't have time to fall in love with an Alpha right now.

*

A non-shifter Alpha/Omega love story with mpreg, a single widower Omega dad, an Alpha who cannot knot, emotional issues, two adorable identical twin boys, and an HEA.

Some characters from "Trust No Alpha" make appearances in this novel, however, this book is a standalone read.

OMEGA CHATTEL
The Omega Misfits Book 5
Wendy Rathbone

At Zilly's Chattel Farm, Alli is seen as an upstart Omega. But in reality, he is the victim of a brutal house-dad who wants to control him. Threatened with being institutionalized when he turns eighteen, Alli runs away.

Tarin is an Alpha who runs a small school from his own home for wayward Omegas. Three or four students at a time are all he can handle and his home is full. But when he meets Alli on the streets, he is compelled to bring him home.

Alli wants a better future for himself, better than selling himself on the streets, so he agrees to be a student, when what he really wants is Tarin himself. Tarin doesn't sleep with his Omega students, and the one exception he made broke his heart.

But Alli is persistent. And not only does Tarin have a weakness for broken young men, there seems to be a spontaneous bond forming between them The combination is turning hotter faster than they can keep up.

Non-shifter omegaverse, fated mates, age gap, virgin, knotting/bonding, high steam, HEA.

THE SLAVE PALACE
Wulf and Locke
WENDY RATHBONE

Conquered. Captured. Sold as a pleasure slave.

After being taken as a prisoner of war, Wulf fights his captors and is sold as a One-Night Thrall to be used and abused, then put to death. He is purchased by a high ranking master of the famous Slave Palace. Why Locke buys him, Wulf has no clue, but something about this master is intriguing.

Instead of abuse, Wulf is plied with luxuries he has never known by a man who actually seems to respect him.

Jaded. Looking for a challenge.

Eminent Master Locke takes on a bet with his best friend that he can't train and tame a dangerous One-Night Thrall in ten days. But something about this slave stirs him like no other before. All bets aside, Locke has the urge to keep Wulf, as well as save his life. But Wulf is fierce, unwilling, and his consent papers have been forged. If Wulf doesn't soon submit to his role as a slave, he will be sent to death as a prisoner of war.

A sweet, slow-burn love story taking place on an alternate contemporary Earth where owning pleasure slaves is legal.

The Imposter Prince
Wendy Rathbone

His love for an enemy prince threatens his very life.

Dare does not mind serving the spoiled and cruel Prince Darius. Growing up with him, Dare does everything for Darius including homework, bed play demands, and even doubling for him as the prince grows too paranoid to face even the smallest of crowds.

But everything changes in a single moment when Dare, while posing as Darius, is abducted by the enemy.

A captive in a new and hostile land, Dare meets another prince who seems just as indulged and rotten as Darius— until Dare gets to know him, until they fall in love. Against his will, Dare must continue to play the role of Prince Darius for real, or risk everything: his love, his land, and his very life.

His only chance for survival is to keep a secret from the one he loves, a secret that is also killing him.

A male/male, enemies to lovers novel of mad kings, troubled princes, abduction, fevers, cold dungeons, warm hearths, comfort, wine, and true love.

BUYING YOU
Wendy Rathbone

It's one thing to be a beautiful cover model on billboards, buses and magazine covers. It's quite another to be sold as one.

Prized for his looks, Dane knows it's shallow, but he is on his way to having it all. It feels good to be gorgeous, smart and have top designers from around the world requesting him.

When he returns to his hometown to participate in a small Date-For-Charity auction, it seems harmless enough—until a hooded man walks in and bids higher on him than anyone else. Dane is intrigued but nervous when he finds out the guy has vanished after the winning bid, leaving only a limo behind to whisk Dane off into the night.

Enemies to lovers, opposites attract, and hot steamy nights that challenge two guys' trust issues along with their biggest fears.

SONS OF NEVERLAND
by Della Van Hise

Set against a backdrop of contemporary culture, *Sons of Neverland* explores the universal questions of love, sex and death - the three most crucial challenges every human being must face. Stefan London is a grieving man, suffering through the loss of his young daughter. When he goes to a science fiction convention in the hopes of meeting her friends, he encounters instead a man who is dangerously seductive. Lured into the night, Stefan soon discovers himself in a world where vampires are real, and immortality is only a kiss away.

But the price of eternal life is high, and as his handsome maker warns, "Through my blood you will learn a secret that will compel you to live forever, yet a secret so sinister it will haunt you for that same eternity."

The secret will haunt you, too.

———

A deliciously dark male/male romance. First time, enemies to lovers, love/hate relationship, HEA.

YEAR OF THE RAM
Della Van Hise

Only after Star Commander Morgan Diego becomes an exile as a result of a Galaxy Corps political blunder does he begin to realize how much he valued the companionship of his second in command - the mysterious Lucien, an Alfarian who is more elfen than human, with peculiar powers & abilities which begin to unfold as he, too, realizes what he has lost.

Separated by circumstance from his former life, Morgan is thrust into a world where he must survive by his wits. When he meets a peculiar little old man calling himself Kim Le, Morgan finds himself in a situation where he is required to master The Art - not only a form of human & extraterrestrial martial arts, but a way of living that will alter his life forever.

At the temple, he is introduced to his new teacher, another Alfarian man who begins to steal his heart - a heart which is already promised to Lucien. Torn and conflicted, Morgan struggles with the world he left behind and the world he now inhabits.

Beginning to believe he may never again return to his ship and to the friends and loved ones he left behind, he is all the more frustrated and heartbroken when a new Master arrives at the temple: a man to whom Morgan is immediately drawn both mentally and physically, a man who is strikingly familiar... yet utterly alien.

www.ingramcontent.com/pod-product-compliance
Lightning Source LLC
Chambersburg PA
CBHW060745180626
46818CB00002B/452